Amy Peters still wore her riding dress, a split twill skirt that allowed her to fork a regular saddle. Her eyes spoke of revenge as she silently stepped past Holten into the room, then stood there until he closed the door.

She turned and stared at him.

"Evening," he finally offered.

"Nathan Barlow murdered my father in his sickbed," Amy began. "I *must* go on the posse. I must have revenge."

"That's what started this whole thing," the scout noted. "The Barlows wanted revenge, now I want revenge and so do you. Tomorrow, the men and I'll ride and do them dirt and get the . . . ladies back."

"I'm going, Scout," the young woman announced and turned her sharp features to Holten. Eli felt stirrings in his loins.

"No," Holten finally answered. "You're not going anywhere. It won't be safe out on this hunt."

"My father taught me to shoot, Mister Holten," Amy countered. "Set me up on a hill with a Sharps and I'll plug the bastards at any distance you can name. I'm good with a Winchester and I can outride any man in this town."

"That, I doubt," Eli said flatly.

#14
THE SCOUT

CATHOUSE CANYON
BY BUCK GENTRY

ZEBRA BOOKS
KENSINGTON PUBLISHING CORP.

ZEBRA BOOKS

are published by

KENSINGTON PUBLISHING CORP.
475 Park Ave. South
New York, N.Y. 10016

First printing: March 1984

Printed in the United States of America

This book is dedicated to Douglas Hirt, fellow Western writer and friend.

"To be killed like a pig, by an Apache, seemed pre-eminently dreadful and contumelious."

— John Ceremony, Scout
His own words.

Chapter One

Swathed in his dark blue greatcoat, the infantry guard walked down the short row of cells and hoisted his oil lamp above his head to inspect the huddled prisoners inside the dark holes. The cold of a Kansas fall night creeped through the high, barred windows in the military prison, chilling the long brick building. The guard came to the cell he sought and smiled to its five occupants.

"Well, boys," the soldier jeered as he hefted his .45 caliber Springfield rifle to his shoulder. "Tomorrow you hang."

"No need ta tell us, soljur-boy," Nathan Barlow answered. "We know."

"Look on the bright side, Barlow," the guard bantered back. "If those folks back in Eagle Butte'd had their way, why you'd had a messy ol' lynchin'. Danced most of the day away. The army, now . . . " He squinted and nodded as though confirming to himself the truth of his words, "We do things right." He pointed from under his weapon with a loose finger while the rest of his hand steadied the rifle. "Bein' extradited here was the best thing the territory could've done for ya. We got experts here at Leavenworth, sent up from St. Louis. They'll hang ya the proper way. When that trap opens, yore neck'll snap like a twig. Nothin' ta think about but who's

7

gonna greet ya at the gate; Peter' r Satan."

"The Lord protects his own," Nathan Barlow intoned in pious notes while he handled the converted 1860 Remington .44 Henry rim-fire under his dirty coat. He gritted his teeth and stared coldly at the guard.

"I ain't got not worry there, boy," Barlow continued. "My conscience is clean."

"Not a man to stew over stealin' er murderin', huh, Barlow? I didn't know you was on such good terms with the Almighty."

The prisoner straightened his back and thrust his jaw forward.

"I did what I had ta do. It's like any man who's gonna live out his days in this sinful world."

"After t'morrow, you won't have ta do much of anythin'," the soldier scoffed, ignorant of the shadowy figure that closed in behind him. "Ya know, Barlow, after hearin' the stories about yuh, I think I'll enjoy seein' you an' yer sidekicks hang."

A knife slithered through the guard's blue woolen coat with enough force to pierce flesh and puncture a kidney. The infantryman tried to scream, but he couldn't stop trying to suck in air. Even if he had been able to cry out, a hand grasped tightly over his mouth. Nathan's brother, Jed, dressed in the uniform of the Fifth Infantry, dragged the silenced guard toward a corner.

One of the cell's inmates, Art Hawkins, quickly pulled a piece of a spoon — twisted, straightened, scraped, and pounded into shape — from its hiding place in a niche in the cell's floor. Deftly he slipped it into the iron door's lock and set to work. Three of the hole's internees huddled at the bars and gave encouragement and advice. Nathan Barlow calmly set about gathering

8

his meagre belongings. Jed nervously crouched and studied the prison's hallway.

"Howdy, Jed," Nathan called out.

"Howdy, big brother," Jed whispered back.

The tumblers clanked and fell into place. The door swung open. Five men staggered out, then fell stealthily to the cover of the walls. The inmates of the other cells began to buzz.

"Hey, Nathan Barlow," one condemned man cried out, "take us along."

"Yeah, we got no love of the hangman," a second voice added.

"All you stay quiet!" Hawkins hissed. "Or you'll pay with your lives." A tense silence fell.

Three of the escapees; John Hay, Harry Lemley, and Harlan Bowes, stripped the guard of weapons and valuables, then picked up the body and hauled it into the cell. Nathan Barlow stepped to the entrance of the hole and his steel-blue eyes looked up and down the block. His chiseled jaw tightened for a moment, then he quoted, fervently if inaccurately, from the Bible. "Verily I say unto you, *Thou shalt not kill.* These men deserve their lives, too, boys. Turn 'em out in the name of the Lord." To his brother, he added in a whisper, "It'll provide a nice distraction, too."

Art Hawkins used his improvised lock pick to quickly open the other cells. Under the hard looks of the Barlow gang, the freed inmates remained silent as they clustered in the corridor.

"Y'all head any way you want, once we get outta here," Nate told them. "But anyone who follows us will buy a bullet instead of an army rope."

Then he joined his men as they followed his brother to

9

the end of the dark passageway. They stepped over another dead guard before Jed brought them to a halt, and the experienced bandits split and hugged the walls.

"Any time now," Jed whispered as he handed out revolvers he'd tucked under his greatcoat and stared across the yet-to-be-completed grounds of Leavenworth prison. The other convicts crowded up behind them. The military corrections barracks had been founded five years before, yet the final solid walls only stood to the west, north, and east.

The shadows of pacing guards moved slowly through the darkness. A good-sized fire burned on the open formation field, where deserters and army criminals fell out every morning to be "corrected." The flames threw light on a well-kept set of gallows to the south, the trapdoors heavily oiled, the necktie nooses shaped of solid new rope. The fire also lit rows of supply wagons stored to the southeast. Hawkins looked to Nathan.

"Why'd we ever let that cavalryman join up with us anyway?" he complained in a hoarse whisper.

"Because he could get us to the Twelfth's horses and the Indian's cattle," Nathan countered with a smile. "They'd have brung us a pretty penny, too."

"Kansas probably would've handed us over to the army anyway," Jed added, "after that killin' at Plain ville . . . "

"We did what we had to do," Nathan answered sharply. Further words were interrupted as a squat, solid, red brick building against the west wall lit up like daytime and cracked the air with chunks of wood, rock, and mortar. Ground shock from the explosion nearly knocked the escaping men off their feet. A billow of dust osbscured the wide parade ground.

Instantly the six men scrambled out of the doorway, running crouched toward the low beam that marked the southern boundary of the prison grounds. The other prisoners raced after them.

"The magazine's blown!" an anonymous soldier shouted the obvious, evidence coming at him in bursts of cartridges and chips of red brick. The confusion worked perfectly, Nathan thought. The guards ran for cover, the corporal of the guard rang the triangle to summon the fire brigade and the escaping civilians wound through the army wagons and supplies toward freedom. They encountered only one sentry.

Nathan Barlow grimly aimed his Remington as the surprised soldier wheeled and raised his rifle. The escapee's revolver barked and grimy smoke exploded out behind the lead slug.

It smacked into the guard's throat and blew through the man's spine. The infantryman bounded off his feet and slapped up against his small guard house. The noise went unheeded in the cacophony of ammunition still detonating.

No time to waste. Already the Fifth's non-coms struggled to get order among the fire fighters to control the inferno. The six fugitives dashed out onto the road that led to the small but prospering town of Leavenworth, Kansas, south of the fort. Well aware of the Barlows' ruthlessness, the fifteen men they had released scattered through the fields like a covey of frightened quail.

A few moments later, the gang ran headlong into eight mounted civilians riding up the road toward the fiery barracks.

"What the hell's goin' on?" one Kansan shouted.

"Nothin' much," Jed answered.

The condemned criminals raised their weapons and a cloud of smoke jumped into the air with lances of fire. Four of the riders jerked as horses reared and bolted. The man in the lead rolled like a ball off the back of his horse. Two townies raised their rifles while the remaining pair tried to turn their mounts south.

Too late. Another crash, like a well coordinated volley, burst against the surprised civilians.

One man's hat went spinning into the air along with most of his bloody skull. A .44 slug smacked hard against the last man's chest, its energy expended itself as it burst his heart with hydrostatic shock. One rider held tightly to his mount's reins while it ran wildly from the noise and smoke. The other Kansans bounced or slid from their saddles. The horses broke in all directions.

"Never mind them," Jed shouted as Hawkins ran after one of the riderless mounts. "Follow me."

Quickly they ran another quarter mile, off the road, to a draw where five disheveled men waited anxiously for the arrival of the Barlow gang.

Nathan studied the unkempt group in the clearing as several of his men rushed forward and smothered the fire that burned cheerily in a ring of rocks.

"What the hell ya think we're holdin' heah, a barnraisin'?" Harry Lemley cursed hoarsely at the chinless man in the front of the group, apparently the leader.

"B-but it were cold," the balding man countered.

"So freeze yer balls off," Harry growled. "That damned fire could get them Bluebellies down on our asses."

"Best I could do, Nathan," Jed quietly directed at his brother.

"Ya did well," Nathan answered. "Ya did what ya had

12

to do. The Lord moves in mysterious ways . . . His wonders to perform."

"It'll take a miracle to make high-binders outta this trash," Harry grumbled as he walked with the other men to the horses.

Quickly the escapees mounted. The other men followed suit. Jed introduced the leader of the disorganized greenhorns as "Big Red" Hennessey.

"It sure is a pleasure ta ride with yuh, Mister Barlow," Red gushed as he shook the strong hard hand of Nathan. "There ain't a man in Kansas what ain't heerd of the Barlow gang."

"It's a pleasure, Red," Nathan answered with forced enthusiasm. He kicked at his horse's flanks and got out ahead of the large group of riders. The prison men ached to put some distance between the Leavenworth gallows and themselves, the others nervously studied the countryside, lit by a full moon and the distant fire at the fort. They could see Nathan's outline, his face in shadows.

"Ah'm Nathan Barlow, for all you what don't know me," he started. "Ya helped us break out and I'm much obliged." The gang leader paused and rearranged himself in his saddle. "Ah warn't afraid ta die, even if I'd done nothin' to deserve it. It were the Lord's will Ah escape. Ah done it 'cause Ah got to settle accounts with folks what done me wrong." Barlow looked to the north. "Ah broke out to set things right, not as soon as Ah like, but soon enough. In the meantime, Ah think we can all make some money, keep ourselves comfortable." The rustler leader's finger rose into the sky next to his head.

"But yuh best do like you're told, when I tell yuh to do it, or else Ah'll kill ya on the spot . . . or make you wish

13

you were dead." Another pause to let the clear threat soak in. "Ah plan ta kill me the Marshal o' Eagle Butte, Dakota Territory, some day. Ah figger to take mah pound of flesh from the folks in that sorry excuse fer a town, but most of all, I reckon ta kill me an army scout and trim his balls off an' make a pouch ta carry mah tobacco in." Barlow again looked north for a long time.

"Ah'm gonna kill Eli Holten, or Ah'll die tryin'."

Reluctantly the gang leader pulled his eyes away from the north and pointed his mount southwest. The ten other desperadoes followed him into the dark prairie.

It could get cold in the Black Hills of Dakota Territory. The wind comes howling out of Canada, sucking warmth from the ground and chilling everything and everyone it touches with its frozen fingers. Eli Holten, Twelfth Cavalry chief scout, had found a warm place to stay in Eagle Butte.

The small, tight bundle of simmering heat squirmed in her sleep, her fingers absently sought refuge around Eli's neck, and her breasts and belly brushed against the scout's lean-muscled stomach. A lusty flint threw sparks on Holten's kindling and ignited a glowing flame of passion. It radiated heat into the goose-down quilt the two hid under from the morning cold. Eli's manhood swelled with the thought of the lovely young madam who had taken such a liking to him.

He tried to keep his mind on other things as the consciousness of half-sleep gave way to full, wide-awake clarity from the thrilling touch of Allison Scott's body. She slept soundly, her breath a rhythmic sigh that slipped through full red lips set in a round cherub face, encircled with light blonde hair. He studied the room for a moment, admiring the decor of the second story dwelling above Eagle Butte's Thunder Saloon and Hotel. Although it seemed gaudy with all the mirrors and the red velvet drapes, he could not forget the wonders they viewed in those peer glasses during their night of ecstasy. Then he remembered the reason it looked so garish and that brought him back to the pretty furnace of desire lying next to him.

"Allison," Eli whispered in her ear.

No response. He stroked her naked thighs and whispered louder.

"Allison. You awake?" A light slap on her curved rump and the angel stirred like a waking cat. Her eyes opened to show off two pale blue orbs that dreamily looked up at him.

"Good morning," he offered. Allison's arms tightened around his neck, then suddenly she jumped as Eli's probing prod slid hot and silky across her belly.

"Lord!" Allison gasped. "Again?"

"I don't mean to impose," Eli began.

"My goodness, 'impose, impose'," she countered. "I can't think of a more pleasant way of bein' awakened." She looked appreciatively at the scout's face again. "You must be the most blessed man in the territory."

"I don't know about that," Holten answered humbly.

"I got into this business 'cause I couldn't ever get enough, dearie," Allison cooed with a kiss to his hairy chest. "By then, I'd been banged by little ones and big ones for seven of my fourteen years and for eight more since then, but none of 'em quite like you. I think you might be the first man to wear me out. I wouldn't mind knowin' that feelin'."

Eli let his rough, work-hardened hand slide down the warm front of Allison, across her firm, round breasts, down along her silky cream-colored belly, to the blonde-thatched opening of her eternal furnace, where coals smoldered, waiting only for more fuel. His fingers acted as kindling, urging the cherub's lusty embers to life as he dexterously slid between the hot pink flaps that moistened with anticipation of his penetration. She groaned prettily in a high voice and began to deftly handle his solid manhood.

A sudden small firestorm swept over little Allison, the intense heat causing her to leap and shudder as from a close flame. She cried out as though burned, only to grasp his hand and implore him to continue the exploration of her lubricated hearth. Her legs spread invitingly under the quilt and Eli hitched over and slid between them. His throbbing skin log stood outside the slippery opening of her fireplace, and she urged him to add more fuel to her ever-building fire.

Eli's stoking gently slid into the baking oven, to feel the flames of passion. Allison stifled a cry as her belly muscles contracted with delight. The young madam, all of five foot four, strugged to keep the vents open by spreading her legs even wider, while Eli vigorously fed her moist stove, building toward another, more heated corona than the last.

Suddenly the scout's slick, flesh log caught fire. It burst into tingling flames of desire and his efforts redoubled. Allison bucked with the scathing heat that scorched between her legs. She cried out, her sharp fingers grasping at Holten's back. Eli resisted releasing the fluid that would quench the fire. He hoped to burn with Allison in the eternal heat of their passion.

Pressure built to an irresistible level and, with a sharp cry, Holten dumped his igneous liquid into Allison's pulsating incinerator. The delirium of his release thrilled his quivering body. Allison leapt with the striking force of the explosion and struggled to squelch a scream. The inferno burned on relentlessly between them.

Without losing pace, Eli worked on, plunging into the searing cavern over and over until he felt the vortex growing once more and they ascended the peak together. The pyrotechnics quelled finally, only after reducing to ashes all the hungers they had felt. Eli struggled to capture his breath, and Allison lay almost unconscious, in the wake of the conflagration.

Eli backed off from the searing moist flesh of the horny young angel and thought perhaps she could be a devil in disguise. Allison smiled dreamily up at Eli and snuggled back closer to his side.

"Goin' back to the fort soon?" she asked.

"Not unless I get called back, or until next spring," Eli answered, still struggling for breath. "I sort'a had this idea about goin' down to Texas for the winter."

"I have an idea, too," the young madam answered. "I thought maybe you'd like to stay here with me and the girls."

"I'd like to live to *see* the spring, Allison," Eli protested through a soft laulgh.

"I'm serious," the naughty cherub pressed. "I could take the winter off so's to entertain you proper-like. I make enough off my ladies so I can do that. If I'm not woman enough for you, or you feel like a little variety, why, I've got ten of the sweetest little doves in the Dakotas livin' with me here and they've expressed an interest in this thought of mine."

Eli stared down to the sweet face of Allison, not quite comprehending. It staggered his imagination. Ten luscious soiled doves, all waiting for their turn to pleasure him. He remembered his long, ardent trip from Dodge City to the Mogollon Rim and his senses reeled at the possibilities.

"Oh, Eli," Allison cried as Holten's thoughts made his ever-ready log provide a center pole for the tent forming from the quilt. "You *will* stay."

A loud, solid knock pounded at the door of the room.

"Whoever it is," Eli boomed. "Go away!"

"It's me, Holten," a familiar burnt-sounding voice came back. "Marshal Peters."

"Can't it wait?" the scout appealed as Allison disappeared under the quilt. Almost immediately he felt a moist, gentle, tugging sensation at his swelling loveweapon.

"You really think I like getting up this early, boy?" the marshall answered. "This is important. It's about the Barlow gang."

"Well, damnit, Peters," Eli snapped, his back arching as the rhythmic vacuum pressure became more insistent. "They were supposed to do a midair jig three days ago."

" '*Supposed to*' is right," the voice through the door replied. "I got a telegram from Kansas City. The Barlow gang broke out of Leavenworth the night before their necktie party."

Chapter Two

It had been more than six months ago, Eli thought, as he quickly dressed, much to Allison's consternation. A trooper from the Twelfth Cavalry had deserted and joined the Barlow gang to steal a hundred precious head of army horses. Then, with the information the trooper possessed, the infamous Nathan Barlow and his cut-throat followers rustled more than two hundred head of the cattle Washington had sent to feed and "domesticate" the Sioux.

The Twelfth couldn't move without more horses and the route that the rustlers took circled northwest. After stealing the cattle, the swing continued until the gang headed southwest. They would have gotten away with it, too, the scout admitted grimly, if Eagle Butte's Marshal, Orsen Peters, hadn't spotted them passing in a wide arc on the east side of the Cheyenne River and sent someone to inform the post of the rustled stock. Although the gang was operating out of his jurisdiction, Peters followed until they halted to change the brands on the cattle.

A smile creased Holten's thin lips. When he caught up with Marshal Peters—a rail of a man, tall and painfully lean, his faced scarred from sun, wind, and battles, and a patch over one eye—the Barlow gang, seven men strong, had bedded down at the mouth of a cave overlooking the wide meadow where the stolen herd grazed.

Barlow must have been confident that he'd gotten away clean. Only two men watched the cattle while the others rested and ate. As Barlow napped, Peters and Holten silently captured the sentries and tied them, then posed as the herd guards themselves until the watch change came two hours later. The surprised relief surrendered without a hitch.

With only three men left, the Marshal and the scout walked into the camp two hours before sun-up, woke the sleeping bandits one by one and took the whole gang without firing a shot. Eli couldn't help but chuckle at the sight of those seven men as the Marshal led them into Eagle Butte. He'd never seen a sorrier bunch of bushwhackers.

In the ways of the West, quick justice could be found at the nearest stout tree and the end of a rope. That's how the people figured the Barlow gang should be treated. The average settler could easily figure out that if the Sioux didn't have meat and the army didn't have enough horses, the townsfolk and homesteaders might be victims of it all before everything settled. To the Sioux, all whitemen, except for a few horse soldiers and a scattering of others like Eli Holten, were the same. One white stole from the Oglala and any and all of them had to pay. A necktie party started forming up, and Eli couldn't see himself making enemies to save the likes of Jed and Nathan Barlow.

Marshal Peters wore the badge, though. He stepped in front of the yelling crowd, spread his legs slightly and placed his tall, lean frame between his prisoners and the townspeople. Holten remembered the look that came on the marshal's ugly face. It spit determination. Peters lifted his eyepatch to expose an empty, fluid-dripping, scarred socket underneath, stepped nose-to-nose with the leader of the lynchers and said, "Go away, or I'll kill you."

The lynch mob went away.

Eli thought about this as he pulled on his fringed, buckskin shirt, then took the extra time to strap his Remington .44 and holster to his hip. Only then did he open the door to Allison's room.

Peters stepped in, a scribbled telegram clenched in his gnarled fist.

"This just got here from the fort," the lawman ground out. "The whole Barlow gang escaped three days ago. Jed Barlow planned the breakout from the other side of the walls."

"Damn," Eli cursed softly, studying the piece of paper Peters handed him.

Allison held the quilt to her neck and blushed demurely.

"Mornin' Miss Scott." Peters absently tipped his hat to her.

"Good morning, Marshal," Allison answered.

"They let Jed Barlow go?" Eli broke in as he finished the telegram.

"Didn't ya hear about that?" the marshall responded.

"Hell, no."

"The courts are goin' down the hole in an outhouse," Peters countered. "We caught 'em all red-handed, but they let this one man go."

"You know why?

"Sure," the marshal answered. "We extradited 'em to Kansas so's they could stand trial for murder there. They didn't kill anyone here, so we sent 'em straight ta

Kansas. Nathan Barlow and everyone but his brother did in some folks in Plainville. Since Jed didn't get in on that job, they let him go. Didn't even bother to hold him long enough fer us ta extradite him back here. Then they shipped the rest of 'em to the army's detention barracks at Fort Leavenworth, so's the Kansans wouldn't lynch 'em."

"And Jed broke them out."

"I should'a let the people here hang 'em when they wanted to," Peters admonished himself grimly. "I'll tell ya this . . . those boys are gonna come back here. Nathan Barlow said as much. Said he'd get even with you, me, and Eagle Butte fer humiliatin' him."

Eli opened his mouth to give his opinion and advice when a bullet chunked into the ceiling with a shower of glass, outside a gun roared. Allison screamed as she ducked under the covers. Eli and the marshal crouched, then ran for the door, Holten grabbing his hat off the chair back.

"It's Prebble's bank." The marshall growled.

"Stay down!" Holten yelled back to the young madam.

"Don't worry."

A cold north wind tugged at the facades of the buildings along the single street of Eagle Butte. Peters loped into the open long enough to fall behind a water trough, his Smith and Wesson Top Break .44 drawn and cocked. The scout hugged the wall of the Thunder Saloon and led with his Remington .44 as he leaned around the corner.

One by one, out of the Eagle Butte General Mercantile that doubled as a bank, stumbled four scruffy-looking young drifters. The last one out carried a bulging white sack. They fired their revolvers back into the store. An old codger, who had until then slept through the noise at his watching post on a bench out in front of the building, awoke, startled, and stumbled to his feet. The bandit with the sack jumped with surprise at the sudden movement.

He fired wildly at the gray-haired figure. The lead slug caught the oldtimer in the left eye. It blew off the top of his head, splattering gray watery brain matter through the glass window he stood in front of. Eli's gray-blue eyes flashed with disgust and anger. Old Matt Colter, a man who'd been there before Eagle Butte existed, had been killed.

The drifters' horses bucked and bolted as the riders struggled to get into their saddles. One of the robbers made it up and urged his mount toward the road out of town.

Eli took careful aim and squeezed his revolver's trigger. The two hundred five grain bullet burst from the Remington with a cloud of white gritty smoke and smacked into the rider's left side. The slug cracked through the mounted man's rib cage into his left lung, expended its energy knocking the robber off his horse as if he'd been hit with a sledge hammer. The young drifter fell heavily on the dusty ground. The hoofs of the milling horses pummeled his body.

The marshal's .44 American spoke and spewed smoke and lead toward the panicked desperados. One rider, not yet in the saddle, jerked spastically as a red mushroom blossomed on his lower spine. He slammed into the horse's side, bounced off, fell to his back and stayed there.

The bandit with the white sack gave up on trying to

mount. Instead, he fired a wild shot at the water trough where Peters crouched and ran for the nearest cover, the livery stable at the end of town. Before he could make it, though, he ran headlong into a man dressed all in black, carrying a large leather-bound book, who had stepped out of the barbershop. Instantly the desperate bankrobber grabbed the minister around the neck. With a quick jerk and a gun at the holy man's head, the bandit took a hostage.

"Anybody moves and Ah'll kill the prayer pusher!" the drifter threatened loudly through twisted, rotting teeth. Panic choked his words.

"You harm a hair on Reverend Smith's head," the marshal growled as he came to his feet, "and I'll cut yer balls off an' feed 'em to ya."

"Pa-lease, Marshal," the man in black rebuked. "There are ladies present."

Eli followed the preacher's pointing finger to the balcony above him. The soiled doves of the Thunder Saloon and Hotel watched anxiously out the windows. Peters grimly tipped his hat to them, then went back to the business at hand.

"I'm warnin' ya," the bandit gulped. "I'll kill him."

The robber and hostage got to the center of the dirt main street, then backed, stumbling toward the livery stable. Eli and the marshal closed the distance, although slowed by the threat of another murder. Silently, the entire town's attention focused on the bandit and his hostage.

Suddenly the Reverend took an extra big step back and slammed an elbow into the young road agent's stomach. Before the thief could react, Smith came to his full height, grasped the Bible prayerfully in his right hand and brought it up to his face. The heavy book held firmly in his fingers, he cried out, "Oh dear Lord, take pity on this poor errant sinner at his time of need."

The young gunslinger looked shaken. Surprise crusted his face.

"Huh?" the stunned gunslick blurted.

The Reverend swiftly swung his black book downward, then straight forward and into the desperado's groin. The bandit doubled over and dropped the heavy white sack. Air whooshed through his crooked teeth.

"I was referring to myself, of course," the Reverend primly explained.

In one powerful lunge, Eli cleared the distance between him and the pain-bent robber. The scout slapped the revolver out of the gunslinger's hand, then racked his Remington heavily across his jaw. The would-be stick-up artist fell senseless to the ground.

From every store and shop came the townsfolk, the men leading the way with shotguns and rifles.

"Ol' Mats's dead." The town drunk stumbled to the hitchrail and howled again. "Ol' Matt's dead!"

"He did it," Percevil Prebble, owner of the Mercantile, stood at the door of his store, blood staining his work apron from his wounded arm. He pointed with it to where Eli stood over the downed bandit. "That scalawag the Reverend thumped. He killed Matt."

Reverend Smith had run to where the oldtimer lay and now knelt next to the blood-stained body that still occasionally jerked in its death throes. "Poor Matthew," Smith declared in a mounful tone. "He slept through all my sermons, but he never snored."

Eli took note of a young, black-haired beauty that rushed out onto the street through the crowd. He didn't recognize the tall, willowy filly as any he'd seen in Allison's stable, but the scout hoped he'd overlooked her. The young woman rushed to where Peters stood and dashed Eli's hopes.

"Daddy!" she cried.

"It's all right, Amy," the marshal answered.

"But you've been hit."

The lawman glanced absently to where the young woman motioned and seemed surprised to find a hole in his shoulder streaming blood.

"Damned if I'm not," he marveled.

"I got some good stout rope here in the store," Prebble shouted. "Let's get it and hang ourselves a murderer."

"Nobody move!" the marshal boomed. He stepped quickly to where Eli stood over the stirring young drifter on the ground.

"Marshal . . . " Prebble began to protest. Peters lifted his eyepatch and everyone cringed away, except for Holten.

"Why do you always do that?" Eli asked.

"I can see better," the marshal snarled.

Peters turned in a circle over his prisoner to face the gathered townsfolk.

"Now you all listen up, 'cause I don't like repeating myself. There's not gonna be no lynchin' in *my* town. We're gonna have a trial, like civilized folk, then we're gonna have a verdict come down, like the law says, and *then* we'll hang the son-of-a-bitch, all legal and proper."

"Marshal," Eli suddenly broke in, realizing they'd all forgotten something. "There were four of 'em. Where's the other one?"

A second of frozen silence let the sensitive ears of the scout hear hoofbeats. Instinctively he looked in the direction from where the sounds came.

A small cloud of dust rose from the east, then disappeared in the rugged, wooded country of the Black Hills.

"There he goes!" Eli shouted.

"Let's go, Holten," Peters ordered, walking toward the livery stable.

"Oh, no, you aren't," Amy Peters protested. "You're bleedin' and you're goin' to the doctor's."

"Best that you stay here, Marshal," Reverend Smith whispered in the lawman's ear. "There might be a lynchin' if you leave town."

"But that fool's gettin' away!" Peters snarled in his deep, bass voice. He looked at Eli.

"Boy," the marshal announced and pointed at the scout. "You've just been deputized."

"Now hold on . . . " Eli began.

"You plannin' to stay in this town fer any length of time, Holten?" Peters asked lazily as he leaned his patchless one-eyed face up to the scout.

"Yeah," Eli answered back, sticking his face the rest of the way to the marshal's. "Are you?"

"Please, Mister Holten," pretty Amy pleaded, her liquid blue eyes pulling Eli's away from her father's gaze. The scout's loins warmed as she spoke. "Won't you go after that blackguard? If you don't, father will."

Eli stared deeply into Amy's warm, luscious face, smiled and took off his hat.

"For you, ma'am, I will."

"We haven't had the pleasure of an acquaintance, Mister Holten," the man in black put in. "My name is Ezekiel Smith. I promise you I'll organize a posse and catch up with you in no time."

27

Eli gave the holy man a quick glance, then looked back at the slowly waking desperado.

"Yeah," he said finally. "I bet you will."

The marshal walked over to the would-be bankrobber, who had come to a sitting position.

"What's your name, boy?" Peters demanded grimly.

"Who wants to know?" the defiant young drifter snarled, rubbing his jaw and groin at the same time.

The lawman leaned down and grimaced into his prisoner's face.

"The man who's gonna make you eat your own balls."

Sincere fear came into the prisoner's expression. "Matthew Blackwell. You ain't gonna let them lynch me, are you?"

Peters smiled and didn't answer.

"Who rode out of town? What's his name?"

Blackwell hesitated for only a moment.

"My brother, Bart." Blackwell's bravado bubbled up for a brief instant. "He's gonna come back and bust me out."

"That'll just get ya both killed," Peters told him matter-of-factly.

Allison, in a light morning dress and heavy boots, dashed from the Thunder Saloon. Eli again felt the flush of warmth from his love of beautiful women and glowed at the image of the lovely maiden rushing out to greet her conquering hero.

To Eli's chagrin, though, the youthful madam ran to the arms of the equally young Reverend Smith.

"Oh, Ezekiel," the soiled dove cooed. "You were so brave."

"You're too kind, Miss Allison," the Reverend said through a nervous smile, then added, "God guided my hand."

"Halleluiah!" angelic Allison squealed with delight. Then she smiled devilishly. "Sometime you'll have to come up and let me show my appreciation for your bravery."

Reverend Smith blushed, but his smile grew from ear to ear as he pulled his black, floppy hat from his head. "I don't think so, Miss Allison, but I appreciate the offer."

Allison didn't seem offended. She smiled coyly and pressed on. "Someday, you're going to change your mind, Mister Smith. And you'll purely love my attentions."

Allison giggled like a little girl, twirled, and gave Eli a wink, then headed back toward the Thunder Saloon and her festive business.

"I rightly do love that gentle lady," Smith sighed to no one in particular. He straightened up and his voice trembled with religious zeal. "And someday, I'll *save* her from her sinful ways."

Eli said nothing, though his eyes narrowed to slits and his jaw tightened. Smith turned to Eli, blushed crimson, then lowered his eyes. He raised them again to meet the scout's.

"But not *too* soon."

"You better git goin', Holten," Peters interrupted. "The sooner you get back, the sooner you can go about yer own doin's."

"Thank you again, Mister Holten." Amy Peters leaned toward the scout as she walked by, her eyes showing her appreciation. "Please, do be careful."

Eli watched the lovely, swinging form of the marshal's daughter as she headed up the street.

"Holten." The lawman broke into the scout's wandering imagination. "As you know, I really like you."

Eli shot Peters a quick glance, not knowing if the tall, gangly marshal was building up to a joke.

"But that's mah daughter you're porkin' in your mind," Peters continued. "To my knowledge, my little Amy's never been with a man." He leaned closer to the scout with his eyeless socket still exposed. "And that's a fable I care to feed."

"Would you put that damned patch back where it belongs?" Eli growled as he slapped his floppy hat onto his head. "You look disgustin'."

Chapter Three

Nathan Barlow studied the soddy from a slight rise. Out front, a white-haired old-timer gleefully tortured a fiddle, while a middle-aged man, two younger men, and an older woman clapped their hands to a pretty girl's jig, who, in a bright cotton dress, whirled and danced in front of them. The music drifted lightly up the hill.

Art Hawkins scratched at his hardening tool.

"I haven't had a piece of poontang in six solid months, Nathan," he announced.

"Neither have I, Art," Barlow replied.

"Damn it, boss. None of us've had a decent bit of tail!" Harry Lemley added desperately. "That purty little thing down there could take care of all of us."

"We gonna get some pussy?" Red queried. "Damn, on the lam and we go get ourselves some lovin'. That's the Barlow Gang!"

"Shut up," Jed Barlow growled. "Nathan hasn't said we're doin' anythin'."

"Please, Nathan," Harlow Bowes begged. "It's somethin' I need."

"There's sure to be food, and maybe ammunition," Jed offered.

The leader of the outlaws didn't speak for a moment, while the fiddle music and clapping drifted up to the eleven fugitives. Finally, Nathan sighed.

31

"A man's gotta do what he's gotta do," he said. "Jed you take Art, John, Harry, and Harlan around back. Stay out of sight, come up behind them. We'll ride in from the front. While they're watchin' us, you take care of 'em."

Excitement could barely be concealed as Jed and the four gang members rode off and headed east. The five new men waited for the signal. Fifteen minutes later, Nathan saw his brother's detachment walking their horses up behind the dirt-colored soddy.

"Time to go Red," the older Barlow announced.

"Damn!" The new man hooted. "Let's go get some pussy!"

"Gentle now," Nathan urged. "No need to make a circus outta this."

The six desperados ambled toward the sodbuster family. The fiddle wailed to a forlorn halt as the four men rose warily, and the mother guided her daughter into the low dirt structure. No sooner had the women closed the door than Jed and his hidden outlaws inched around the building, unseen by the farmers.

The old man reached casually for an ancient, front-loading shotgun against the side of the pioneer's dwelling. The two boys gathered up well-kept Sharps carbines from where they had them propped against the fence around their home. Nathan ignored the preparations. Instead he smiled and touched the brim of his Stetson.

"Howdy," he called out. "We heard the music from the top of the hill. Sorta caught our curiosity."

"Just a little birthday party, stranger," the father answered coolly. "Pretty much a family thing."

"Just as well," Nathan responded.

A sudden explosion of gunfire shook the rustic scene as five men from behind and the side, then all eleven bandits emptied their weapons into the four settlers.

The old-timer's shotgun discharged into the sky. The weapon's owner popped with bloody mushrooms across his chest and belly, smashing him to the dusty yard of the homestead. He screamed in indignation while he struggled for a moment more on the ground. The middle-aged man didn't have a chance to touch the huge Merwin & Hulbert, .44-40 that protruded from his belt. A 250 grain, .45 slug bit deep into his neck and blew his jugular vein apart. His two sons fired their weapons, one round burning a shallow groove in the heel of Red's hand. The boys fell with slugs in their chests. One, the older of the sons, struggled to regain his feet. Jed Barlow stepped up behind him, leveled his Smith & Wesson American at the base of the sodbuster's head and squeezed the trigger. The boy's face splattered messily on the ground before him.

Quickly Hawkins and Lemley kicked open the door to the soddy and dashed in.

Screaming and sounds of desperate struggle issued from the interior of the earthen home. Shortly, each man came out with a thrashing woman over a shoulder. Hawkins ripped the front of the young girl's cotton dress to reveal half formed, cream white breasts.

"Got a load a them tits, boys!" he cried, desperate lust choking at his breath.

Red had slid off his horse, run over to the twitching body of the young settler who had shot him and began kicking the boy.

punches to her stomach and a teeth-jarring blow to her jaw solved that inconvenience.

Nathan took his turn and his time on the mother. He thought about how he, though only forty, couldn't get real satisfaction from the young ones. An older woman with experience offered him the kind of mature emotion he needed. Barlow looked down at the shattered, bloody mouth of the woman, then forced her head around to look into her eyes as they registered each thurst of his penis into her body. No mere child could muster such passion. Convulsively he climaxed and sated his manly urge.

Julie had stopped screaming. Only desperate whimpers breathed from her lips now, a teeth-clenched groan for each thrust of the new man that rent her savaged womb. Soon even that stopped. The thoroughly raped virgin had passed out from the pain. Black blood, not from her maidenhead, began to coat the ripping lances that tore at her flesh.

The eleven bandits' nervous energy flowed out of them, guffaws and maddened shrieks of laughter broke down to gleeful grunts of pleasure.

Nathan waited until some of Red's boys finished up on the mother, stood over her violated, exhausted form and spoke with his sincerest voice.

"Ma'am," he started. "Ah just wanted ya ta know, yuh was might good. Ah thought Ah'd thank ya an' yore daughter for the time an' effort yuh spent on us t'day."

Through blurry eyes that stared disbelievingly up from her tear-streaked face, Julie's mother studied the murderer of her husband and sons, the raper of her daughter.

"I'll see you swing for this, you scum," she choked out, even as Red continued to rape her Julie. "Somehow I'm gonna see you pay."

Barlow's appreciative face faded into a sad, grim smile.

"Ah know you would, ma'am," he said simply, then pulled his revolver and placed the muzzle to her forehead and blew her skull open. The devoted mother bounced away, her death spasms a grim parody of sexual orgasm.

Red still rutted atop Julie, his eyes riveted on the twitching form of her mother.

"We gonna do that ta little Julie here?" Red asked excitedly as he set his rhythm on the unresisting girl.

"Won't be necessary," Jed said grinning, and began to roll a cigarette. "Ah figure she's been dead fer the last twenty strokes or so."

Red's face lost all expression, then all color. He turned, horrified, to stare at the bleeding, battered body that already looked pale and drained. The two-bit rustler struggled up, gagged, staggered to his feet and away from the dead girl.

"Why the hell didn't you tell me?" he bellowed.

"Why ruin all yore fun?" Hawkins asked reasonably as he hitched up his pants.

The desperadoes turned their attentions to the belongings of the simple homestead, gathering weapons and food together, as well as two horses to carry the booty.

"We gonna kill the milk cow?" Red asked. "We caint take her with us."

"Why kill it?" Lemley inquired.

Red thought a moment, then shrugged.

"I-I don't know," he stammered. "Somehow seems wrong ta leave anythin' alive."

"Leave her, Red," Nathan answered, his morality offended at the pointlessness of killing a good cow. "Might be someone else can use her."

The band of killers turned their backs on the butchered family and rode due south. On a nearby rise, Nathan and Jed halted a moment to study the carnage they had left behind. The elder Barlow sighed sadly.

"Ya know something, Jed?" Nathan finally volunteered.

"What's that, Nate?"

"The world jest ain't fair," Barlow said grimly, then reined his horse around. "It's downright cruel."

The outlaws continued south until they came to a fast flowing, shallow creek. Nathan Barlow brought the group to a halt.

"Red," he demanded sharply, and dug a piece of jerky from his saddle bag. The dim-witted outlaw rode quickly to his leader's side.

"Yes sir, Mr. Barlow," Red answered.

Still looking away, studying the horizon, Barlow offered Red a piece of the dried meat. Red took this as an offer of friendship, and gratefully accepted.

"We got some problems, Red," Nathan started. "Sorta hoped you and your boys could help solve a couple of 'em."

"If'n we can, Mister Barlow," Red complied.

"Call me Nate, boy," Barlow urged with a crooked smile. Red grinned in imagined camaraderie.

"What Ah'm thinkin' is," Barlow continued, "we don't

have enough horses ta get all the way to Mexico for the winter, not ridin' hard we don't. And we don't have enough money. Besides, by now, I'll bet the army and half the country is on the lookout for us, a band of men eleven strong stands out. They catch up to us, we'll all hang."

Red's slow mind began to make sense of what he'd been told. Anxiety crept into his face.

"Whut are we gonna do?" he begged.

"I gotta plan in mind thet could get us outta the territory and down inta Texas," Barlow explained. He pointed up the clear running creek.

"You take your men west about a mile. You'll find a small spread called the Broken Bow. We stole about a hundred head a cattle there, before we. . . ah. . . had ta leave Kansas."

Nathan shot a glance at his brother, who stared a moment into his brother's eyes, broke the gaze, then looked east, along the creek.

"You go there and grab maybe three horses each. Hell, nobody'll bother ya, no matter what the brand. If ya get a chance though, change the brands. Come ta think of it, make a point of it. We head east, along this creek." Barlow leaned toward Red. "We got a—little stash a loot near Bonner Springs. We'll grab some more horses and then head south, meet ya in Coffeville."

Barlow looked back over his shoulder. "Harlan," he cried. "What's the name o' thet whoorhouse in Coffeville? The one ole 'Cap' tole us about?"

Harlan looked perplexed for a moment, his eyes darting from Nathan to Red, then back to Nathan.

"The Coffeville Comfort House," he finally said.

"That's it!" Barlow roared heartily, winked at Red and smiled.

"Just tell Miss Woo that Nathan Barlow sent ha. She'll make sure you get treated right."

"That's great," Red hooted.

"Come spring, we'll head north again, and introduce ourselves to Eagle Butte." Barlow straightened in the saddle. "Ah'm a right patient man when it comes ta gettin' even."

"Stay in the creek," Barlow warned. "Lose those tracks. Hit the Broken Bow Ranch, an' we'll meet ya at Coffeville."

"Damn right!" Red shouted. He touched spurs to his horse and urged it down to the water. "C'mon boys," he shouted to his men. "Let's get ta gitten'!"

The four young scum whooped and splashed into the water to join their leader, waving to the six killers left on the bank.

Jed barlow began rolling a cigarette as he watched Red and his men disappear up the draw.

"Nate," Jed started as the last man rode out of sight. "You know as well as Ah do, if those boys stop to fix the brands on those ponies, that hardcase crew from the Broken Bow will be on them like stink on shit. They'll be markin' their own graves."

"And if they go to Woo's place," Harlan threw in, "an' tell her you sent them, she'll tell 'Cap' Williams, and he'll arrest them fer jest admittin' they know ya."

"Men," Nathan announced as he turned to lean on the rump of his horse. "You really didn't think I was gonna make you ride with shit like that." He turned his mount east, then added over his shoulder. "I don't think they'll

39

make it past that bunch at the Broken Bow, but no matter who catches 'em, if any survive, they'll be tellin' that we're headin' for Coffeeville, then aimin' fer Mexico by way o' Texas. We're headin fer Kansas City fer a meetin', then on ta Eagle Butte."

The Barlow Gang, now only six men, rode past Bonner Springs, to a small abandoned ranch house far outside town. From a well Nathan pulled a canvas sack, hidden there nearly two years previously. Out of the bag they retrieved thirty-five hundred dollars in gold coin and a waterproofed container that held a passbook to the First Territorial Bank of Kansas and a Bible.

In Rosedate, a few miles outside Kansas City, Nathan and Jed met up with nine men, cutthroats and gunslingers in clean new store clothes, with shaved faces or groomed beards and moustaches. They retired to a simple town saloon serving good whiskey and beer and a free lunch of cold cuts, pickled pig's feet and home-baked bread.

The Barlow brothers sidled up to the bar where one well-dressed man stood, nursing a brew.

"How are ya, Jed?" the man asked.

"Real good, Tony," Jed answered. "This here's muh brother, Nathan. Nathan, this is Tony Cooper, and those boys over there is his hired guns."

"You ought to know, Jed," Tony quipped. "You hired 'em."

"I found the best ta find the best," Jed responded, and winked at the professisonal shootist. "Got a hold a Tony 'fore I went up to Leavenworth."

Jed leaned to Nathan's ear.

"Already paid him five hundred."

"I got fifteen hundred more that says they're still hired," Nathan told the gun hand.

"I don't know how you think we're gonna get from here to South Dakota with every law man in Kansas and the army huntin' fer ya, Barlow." Cooper said. "But for that kind a money, I'm willin' ta try, an' if ya do, I'm figurin' you're a goddamn genius, and I'll go where ya say."

"Good." Barlow smiled. "You're gonna help me a lot."

Chapter Four

A light drizzle began to fall shortly after Eli left town. Two days later the gluelike mud still sucked at his Morgan's hooves, though Sonny traveled well. Blackwell turned southeast shortly after leaving town, Eli less than an hour behind. The would-be bank robber crossed the Cheyenne River near Wasta early the next morning, and headed, with swings and attempts at covering his trail, northeast. Holten realized shortly, that at this rate, Blackwell would enter an area where many Sioux were camped as they migrated toward their winter grounds. The second day dawned with drizzle still falling. Toward the end of the day, nothing had improved, except that Eli thought he would catch up with the fugitive shortly.

Sonny plodded patiently, while his rider held on, feelilng a growing anger at Amy Peters.

Why the hell was he out here in this rancid weather? Because some pretty piece of fluff with big blue eyes, batted them in his direction, that's why. Did she offer him anything in return? A peck on the cheek? An invitation to dinner? Instead of soaked to the bone with a chilling wind to his back, Eli could be in a nice warm bed, dry and relaxed, little Allison propped up on top, her tiny magic fingers twined through his chest hair, inspecting his many battle scars, clucking over each one before she kissed it, working her way down to the one never-wounded part of his body. She'd start to kiss the ever-swelling shaft, sucking and licking until her passion and her jaw opened wide. . . . .

Branches crackled to the scout's right; Eli had let his mind stray too far. Instantly Eli ducked, twisted to the right, hunting for a target as his hand flicked to the smooth-worn walnut of his Remington's butt.

In the same instant, a rifle broke the quiet of the countryside, and Holten felt a bolt of fire kick his saddle.

The bullet ricocheted off the cantle and burned across the usually stout-hearted Sonny's sensitive upper withers. The animal leaped at the excruciating pain and threw Eli from his saddle. Eli rolled hard to the right, onto his shoulder as he hit. For a moment the animal panicked, spooking toward cover further down the road.

"Sonny!" Eli shouted from his prone position as he drew the Remington and fired in the direction of the bushwacker's attack. The animal seized control of itself, turned fiery eyes to its master and held its ground.

A revolver fired and its slug smacked the dirt in front of him as he scrambled to the open side of the Morgan to drag out his Winchester .44-40. A painful grating sensation in his shoulder told him he'd rolled too hard to his right. For a moment he wrestled with the pain, but a blast from the assassin's short gun made Eli hunt for cover. He slapped the horse's rump, then scrambled for safety. Selecting his best option he sprinted for a lone pine tree on the side of the road.

The ground swept solidly up, like the forested ramparts of the Black Hills. There, the umbrella of trees could get so thick that the earth below never saw light, and the terrain often jutted high in the air. The Black

Hills lay west of the Cheyenne River, but this part of Dakota could surely pass for a piece of the Sioux's sacred mountains.

Bart Blackwell had chosen a good ambush spot, Eli had to admit. The fugitive stood on high ground with lots of cover to the right of the road. Rocks, boulders, and brush offered many opportunities for fire and movement. Eli, on the other hand, now sat behind a lonely pine on a flat surface, the nearest alternative cover a good hundred feet away; nothing but bunch grass covering the space between the single pine and better protection. Yes indeed Eli thought, the boy had chosen well.

Bark splintered off the tree Eli lay behind. The scout hunkered down to the side of the tree, studied the route to the better, thicker cover, then concentrated on his opponent.

The bushwacker must have a single shot rifle, Holten reasoned. And in a big caliber, probably a .45-70. A Sharps was improbable, except for Civil War carbines converted to cartridge. The rifle had a sharp report, which indicated a long barrel. That ruled out the Sharps. More than likely it was a Remington or a Springfield. Holten favored a Remington, because he hadn't heard the clack of the trap-door action on a Springfield.

Eli quickly visualized the loading drill for a Remington, trying to get the count down on how long it would take to reload. Not long. In a good ambush position, Bart Blackwell had a revolver lying next to the more accurate weapon. Eli prepared himself to run, deliberately drew fire, slammed two quick shots into the windward side of a gray-white puff of rifle smoke, then made his move.

44

Running headlong, Eli scrambled for the thick cover to his left.

Before he'd gotten more than a few yards, the hidden rifle blasted. An unseen foot booted Holten in the ass with enough power to spin him from his feet. He landed in a prone firing position and squeezed two more careful shots at his assailant. He could hear the bushwacker whoop with confidence.

Quickly Eli figured the distance to the better cover. Blackwell would be reloaded and shooting at the scout again, and now Holten couldn't run. Eli turned and started back toward the pine. He stumbled toward the only source of cover nearby and realized at this rate, the ambusher would be reloaded and have the scout in his sights in a second. He forced more speed, keeping the count and drill of the Remington in his head. When the number came up, Eli froze.

The five hundred grain slug tore a patch of air out of the world two feet in front of Eli's nose. Its shock wave slapped at his face. Holten lurched forward again to the cover of the pine.

The scout had trouble stopping the bleeding. He pressed a clean handkerchief against the wound and took solace in the fact that the bullet did not remain. If he tried to return fire, though, he'd have to take pressure from the two gaping holes.

Another slug pummeled the ground next to where Eli hid.

"Hey, lawman," a heckling voice shouted down from the hill. "Looks like you're a dead man ta me."

"You think so, huh, boy?" Holten hollered back. "Why don't you come down here and we'll talk about it?"

"Oh no," Bart laughed back. "I like it right heah, jest

waiten fer ya ta bleed ta death, seein' if Ah cain't speed up yore heah-aftah with a couple a well placed bullets."

Blackwell chortled gleefully, sighting his rolling block .45-70 on an object that looked like a part of the scout. The big five hundred grain slug spatted dirt on Eli's leg.

"Did Ah skeer ya?" the ambusher jeered as he cocked the Remington's hammer and rolled the breech-block down to extract his empty brass.

"Not near as scared as your brother is back at Eagle Butte, Bart," Eli countered. "He says you are going to come back and bust him out."

"Damn right," Blackwell boasted in reply, although actually this was the first time the thought had crossed his mind. With a more grim determination, the bushwacker moved to his left to get his target into his sights again.

Eli took the pressure off the bandage long enough to aim his rifle and get a shaky round off. The slug snapped past Blackwell's head. Bart fell unceremoniously to the ground.

"Two can play this game, Bart." Eli bellowed.

The fugitive angrily came to his feet and fired with determination. The bullet smacked into Holten's left boot, blowing off the tip a fraction of an inch from the scout's toe. Eli jerked with the impact. It sent searing pain through his otherwise numb butt. Holten pulled his legs up against his stomach and checked the tingling foot for damage, trying to present less of a target.

"Bet that smarts, huh lawman?"

"I ain't no lawman, boy," Eli responded. "I'm just a member of the posse. Eli Holten is the name."

That would give the little bastard something to think about, the scout thought. Eli chastised himself for rushing so far ahead of the townsmen. He pressed more of the stubby .44-40 cartridges into his Winchester, thanking providence Blackwell had not chosen to take full advantage of the big .45-70's superior range and accuracy.

Holten had planned to drag the desperado back for trial all by himself; now he paid for hurrying and being so cocky. His professional trailcraft should have made the job easy, but Eli knew he had violated the first rule of scouting: stay alert and plan ahead. The little son-of-a-bitch would never have gotten him here if the scout had not been daydreaming of Allison's deft administrations and her willingness to share.

Eli tried a new tactic to wrap his injury. The bullet hadn't cut deep but followed a strange angle, where Holten had trouble getting pressure on the wound. He used his gunbelt to get the exit wound, but that left the entrance hole still gaping and bleeding freely. The numbness that first came with the projectile's impact yeilded to a swelling pain.

"What posse?" the bushwacker shouted after a long pause. Then with false bravado, "I got a clear view of yore back trail. There ain't no one comin', *Mister Eli Holten*!

"I was scouting ahead," Eli answered calmly. "They'll be along d'rectly."

Bart Blackwell nervously glanced along the road that could accommodate a wagon, then back over his shoulder. If a posse heard the shooting, they'd slip into the cover he enjoyed, only from above and behind him. They could be closing in on him right now.

No, he'd hear them, though the thought did little for his jangled nerves. Bart told himself that he might be a loser in some ways but he was a fair hand at woodcraft;

he knew he'd hear them. All the same Bart quickly moved his horse closer to his ambush so he wouldn't have to run so far in the event the posse did show. A quick shot into the tree that sheltered his target assured him his prey was still there.

"Y're a liar!" Bart accused. "Y'er jes' tryin' ta get me ta break an' run!"

"Suit yourself." Holten replied. He wondered how far back the posse could be. A day? Two? If the ambusher kept his head, Eli would die before nightfall. He'd bleed to death.

Nervously Bart wiped at dry lips as he studied the road. He didn't dare fire any more shots that would locate the ambush site, if there really were a posse. All he had to do was finish off this one man below. Then he could move on quickly and the posse would be tied up with the body. Besides, the bushwacker began to figure this posse scout might be the only one he had to worry about. Kill the man and solve Bart Blackwell's problems.

The bushwacker made the kind of mistake that a coward makes under pressure. He gave up his partial advantage of range and moved into easy reach of Eli's rapid-firing Winchester.

Slowly he began to work himself to the right, moving down the rise, hiding stealthily behind brush and a fallen tree.

Eli searched the hillside, nearly inviting a bullet, to locate the fugitive. Nothing. A fearful possibility crossed the scout's mind. Quickly he turned to his left.

For a long time he stared silently, unmoving, waiting as the slowly shimmering trees and brush swayed in the wind. Then, a bush moved, almost imperceptibly wrong to the flow of the cold wet breeze.

If Blackwell made it to the road, Eli figured, the bandit would be close enough to get a clear shot at him from the cover of a huge cluster of boulders.

Holten rolled around the pine, stopped on his belly and brought the Winchester to bear. Mercilessly pounding pain ricocheted through his body. For a moment he struggled to catch his breath. He steadied his rifle and aimed for the slight shiver of motion in a clump of brush a little above the rocks at the side of the road.

Then the scout waited, trailing the furtive telltale signs of Blackwell's movement.

Bart eased into the rocks, smiled as he figured how much closer he was now, then peeked over the top of the boulder he crouched behind.

The Winchester barked, a two hundred five grain slug tore in a straight deadly path for Blackwell's exposed head.

Providence protected the young blackguard that day, though. The wind pushed a piece of brush into the path of the deadly chunk of lead with Bart Blackwell's name on it and caught the slug in its flight, deflecting it upward.

Splinters of the saving shrub dug into Blackwell's face, and the slug blew his hat off. The hot lead bounded off a flat stone and moaned away.

Bart screamed his terror at the near miss. He fell back on the ground, heart racing, his blood suddenly pounding in his ears.

Eli jacked the lever action Windhester to chamber a fresh round, pointed at where the scream came from and waited again.

Blackwell struggled to his feet and started running

49

wildly back up the hill, stumbling several times in his panic to reach the top.

Eli suddenly felt incredibly weak. His hands trembled as he tried to steady his sights, but the pain forced everything else out of his mind. The roll he'd made to cover had ripped the makeshift bandage open and placed incredible torque on the wound. For a moment, the scout blacked out.

Bart struggled desperately to catch his breath. He gasped and sucked in air until he thought his lungs would burst. The man below had to be a sorcerer. How could Holten have known where he had gone? Thoroughly shaken, Bart feverishly started to gather up his belongings, a plan forming to run as fast, and as far, as his horse would let him.

The sound of hoofbeats roused Eli from his pain-filled stupor. He called to the faithful Sonny, who ambled over to sniff his master's wound. Holten grabbed the trailing reins and started pulling himself up the side of the pine, swearing he'd get the little shit, Bart Blackwell.

The scout's legs collapsed under him. Blood soaked the back of his pants, and he felt weaker and more nauseous than he'd ever been before in his life.

It was a damn flesh wound he told himself. He'd been hit much worse before.

And nearly died from them he recalled.

Suddenly it seemed much colder. His hands felt numb. He had no sensation in his fingers. New ripples of nausea reeled in his stomach.

He had to get on his horse. Sonny sniffed at Eli, concern filling the brave, intelligent animal's face. Holten reached out to grab the saddle horn and fell heavily to the ground.

Hoofbeats sounded nearby. A thousand things crossed the struggling man's mind. Had Blackwell come back? Did the posse press harder along, hearing the shots?

Holten saw hooves land next to him. With every last ounce of his strength he pulled his Remington and rolled over.

Above him sat a bronzed man, bare chested in the cold. He wore buckskin leggings and rode a high Indian saddle. Feathers decorated his head and he stared grimly down at the prone and bleeding Holten.

No, Eli thought, it wasn't the posse.

Chapter Five

Red Hennessey and his four men laughed and joked as they led the string of stolen horses along the trail, bearing southwest through Kansas.

"How long do you figure it's gonna take us ta get ta Coffeville, Red?" Luke asked the leader as he trotted up beside him.

"Give her a couple more days," Red ruminated, glancing back over the little cavalcade. Each man led three horses, stolen from the working string of Broken Bow ranch two days earlier, the same day they had last seen the Barlow Gang. The stolen horses now wore a scabbed over Circle 'D' brand that had been altered from the Broken Bow at the first night camp. Red Hennessey even decided the mythical Circle 'D' was located near Coffeville, Kansas, should anyone ask. The posse had circled around. The trail Red and his boys had taken allowed enough cover to hide the ranch hands of the Broken Bow, augmented by cowboys and ranchers from three other outfits picked up along the way. The owner of the Broken Bow gave the signal, and forty men stepped into the road, instantly surrounding the five rustlers.

"Hey!" Red shouted, his horse shying back. "What's going on here?"

"These here yore hosses, boy?" Broken Bow owner

Arlow Simms asked as he dismounted from his own animal.

"Hell yes," Red retorted. "We're from the Circle 'D' near Coffeville."

Simms stepped to the flank of the animal Hennessey rode, studied the brand there, smiled, then grabbed Red by his chaps and pulled the man from his horse in one mighty heave. The rancher jerked the struggling rustler to his feet and jammed his face next to the altered brand.

"You got ta unnerstand, boy, that I've lost a few hosses in mah time," Simms drawled. "Few years back I got tired of it so I've been slippin' a shiny new dime under each o' my brands. When y'all went over my mark with that runnin' iron to make it match your Circle 'D', that dime gathered heat from the inside. Give it a hour or so an' the image shows right through. Now you look real good, boy, 'n tell me what you see."

Through the skin of the horse he'd been riding, peeking from under the edge of a scab, Red could clearly see the serrated edge of a dime, right down to the 1871 date.

The paddle-wheeler *Selkirk*'s whistle blew a long blast. The docks of Kansas City, Missouri, on the shores of the Missouri River, reverberated with its echo. Passengers and cargo loaders had fifteen minutes to board. Then the *Selkirk* would steam up the Missouri, stopping briefly at the town of Leavenworth, then steam almost non-stop for North Platte, Nebraska.

More than a dozen clean-cut men in new suits and derby hats led their horses, prancing and snorting fear of this noisy monster, onto the main deck of the steamboat. Livery hands took the fine beasts and moved them to the stable area at the stern where hopefully the boat could outrun the smell of offal from assorted horses, pigs, goats, and cattle.

An excited stevedore came running along the shore until he reached the small floating dock.

" 'Ave you heard ze news?" he yelled to the press of people at the rails of the river vessel. "Zey 'ave caught some of ze bastards zat raided zose 'omesteaders in Kawn'zas!" Nathan could barely understand the man's thick French-Canadian accent, though the words made welcome sounds to his ears.

"You mean Barlow and his gang?" the captain of the *Selkirk* shouted down from his pilot house on the Texas deck.

"No zir," the dock-hand replied. He puffed his chest and swaggered at the attention of the river boat's skipper. "Some of 'is men wear caught in ze act of stealing 'orses . . . five of zem, an' before 'ee 'ang zem, zey tol' a ran-cher named Arlow Simms zat ze Barlows a'wir bound for Coffeville."

"Damn!" the captain shouted joyously, slapping the oak railing. "That'll be good news up at Leavenworth!"

From his vantage point on the stern of the passenger deck, Nathan Barlow gave his brother a knowing smile.

"Those coins under the brands is what done it," he chuckled. "I knew Simms wouldn't have no trouble findin' 'em."

"It bought some time Nate." Jed replied.

"Yore a damn genius, Mister Barlow," one of the new guns told him appreciatively.

"That's because Gawd is on my side." Nate answered sincerely. "This here falls under righteous wrath. I will

54

have vengeance, sayeth the Lord!" The leader of the fifteen newly dressed cutthroats felt his jaw tighten as he thought about what he'd do to Eli Holten and Marshal Peters.

If Nathan Barlow could have seen Eli Holten at that moment, he would have felt rather good.

"I not see you for many moons, Tall Bear," Big Wolf, a warrior chief of the Oglala Sioux, said evenly in English from the back of his horse as he studied the man on the ground.

"It has been much too long," Elil answered, trying to keep his voice strong and even.

"We hear shots, then we see white man ride off. Big hurry. We find you were." Big Wolf continued matter-of-factly. The warrior leaned down to get a better look at the scout.

"You not bad hurt, Tall Bear," he noted, a slight rebuff in his tone.

"I have lost much blood," Eli stated.

"Much blood," the mounted Indian admitted. "No stop bleeding, you die."

"*Hoka hay,*" Eli grunted, though it did not seem such a great day for dying. Holten's reply, however, seemed to please Big Wolf.

"That Oglala in you." Big Wolf laughed. "Warrior not fear death."

Eli blinked agreement and licked dry lips.

"You like us fix," Big Wolf finally offered. Only now did Eli notice three other warriors.

"We got big healer in camp," Big Wolf continued as if trying to convince Holten to let them help him.

"Heap medicine."

"I would like that," the scout answered after a moment's pause.

The warriors dismounted and set about to stop the bleeding. They, too, found the angle of entry hard to work with. By stuffing the woundfull of nearly dry moss, they finally did stave the flow of blood. Shortly, they placed the wounded man in the saddle of the powerful Morgan. Riding to each of his sides, they kept him there as they headed west, soon leaving the road.

It seemed to take most of the night to Eli. Actually it lasted nearly an hour. The riders entered the Scared Hoop of the Oglala camp while it was still wide awake, lit brightly by cook fires. Children and camp dogs all howled together at the returning warriors, dashing alongside, seeming to defy the ponies to step on them. Deftly the animals sifted through the greeting party, to halt before a large tipi, its buffalo hide sides covered with symbols of magic and medicine.

The young boys quarreled over who should take the horses as Big Wolf helped Eli from the Morgan.

Holten would have flushed with embarrassment had he the requisite blood. Between the rain and his wounds he felt like a still wet, newly born lamb. His legs wobbled when Big Wolf got him to the ground and another brave took the scout's other side. They half carried him into the lodge and laid him down on a soft bear skin, next to the fire that glowed in a pit near the center of the shelter.

"This Thunder Woman's tipi," Big Wolf explained simply. "She is healer. *Wakan* smiles she live with us this winter."

Eli nodded, his mind clear, but his limbs unresponsive. Some wise old hag that shrilled and stank would nurse him back to health. He hoped she could get him strong so he could go after Blackwell before someone else got to the no-good skunk.

A small figure stepped through the flaps of the conical lodge. Holten looked up to see a young, full-bodied woman, probably in her early twenties, wearing a white doeskin dress, its sleeves decorated with silver hawk's bells. An elk-skin shawl with beautiful quill-work symbols that Eli did not recognize covered her shoulders. Her moccasins and short leggings sported similar odd designs. Her face, however, caught Eli's imagination.

The girl's features could be called plain, except for the light that seemed to emanate from her face, though her eyes were downcast as were any good Sioux woman's around men. Her voluptious body slid under leathern clothing, causing fascinating undulations.

"Thunder Woman!" Big Wolf pontificated, for the first time speaking his native tongue. "This is Tall Bear, chosen son of Two Horns, a chief of forty lodges. He is *Tonweya*, a scout for the American Horse Soldiers. Some person has shot him. He had lost much blood. You will heal him?"

"*Ah-ee*, I shall try to help," the young woman answered softly.

"*Anhe*, you will be all right now, Tall Bear." Big Wolf told the scout and left.

Thunder Woman called in several other women. They stripped the soggy clothing from the wounded man, giggling over the location of his injury and the startling whiteness of his buttocks. Busily they dropped heated stones from the fire into an Oglala "pot," a buffalo stomach held up pouchlike on four poles in one corner of the lodge, and filled half full of water. Thunder Woman ignored the banter. Steam rose from the paunch, and the young healer set about adding dried moss, herbs, and pounded roots to the brew.

The better to spoon hot broth into Eli's mouth, the women rolled him half over and caught sight of his massive organ. Cries of *"Hinu! Hinu!"* were followed by shrieks of happy laughter and bawdy jokes that coupled Eli with the medicine woman.

Thunder Woman flew into an apparent rage and chased her erstwhile helpers from the tent, speaking most disrespectfully for a woman of her obvious youth. The girl leaned over the wounded scout and began to chuckle as she pulled up a bearskin to cover him.

"Those horny old biddies would let you die from exposure just to admire your *sluka*," she said with a grin.

Returning to her pot, Thunder Woman scooped the boiling poultice from the cooking pouch onto a slab of split cedar and carried it to Eli's side, then rummaged in a parfleche for some wide strips of tanned doeskin. Kneeling beside the wounded scout, she tested the temperature of her poultice with a delicate finger, then sat back on her heels to wait. Eli dozed.

Holten started awake when Thunder Woman peeled the robe down to his knees, then she worked the rough bandage loose and poured water over the moss to loosen it. When she plucked the bloody mass off, Eli could contain himself no longer.

"How's it look?" he grumbled.

"You have two holes with a flap of skin over it." she murmured, clinically. "The moss those ruffians stuffed into it had not been boiled, so to remove it all I will have to open the wound. Also there is a very nasty bruise."

So saying, she reached into a pouch at her belt and

produced a piece of blue flint.

"The chipped stone carries a sharper edge than your steel will take," she observed. Then she bent over and deftly sliced open the bridge of flesh between the entrance and exit holes.

"*Unpogapi kilo!*" she exclaimed. "I am pleasantly surprised. The bullet did not cut into the muscle but traveled between it and the skin. You will recover very rapidly."

"Glad to hear it." Eli managed between clenched teeth as the medicine woman proceded to bathe the wound. Then she placed the poultice into the gaping hole, and the sweating Eli nearly choked trying to suppress the agonized scream, then regained the ability to breathe.

"Jesus."

Binding the boiled moss poultice into place was almost an anti-climax, though Thunder Woman did utter a tiny gasp when she saw the size of the scout's magnificent, though flacid organ. Once finished with her ministrations, she pulled the robe up to cover his shoulders, then leaned back and lowered her eyes. Eli gradually became aware that custom had replaced the professional healer and that she desired him to speak.

"Is there something Thunder Woman wishes to ask?"

"Thunder Woman wonders if perhaps Tall Bear might be hungry or thirsty?"

"Tall Bear is thirsty . . . and hungry," he added.

Thunder Woman smiled softly and left the lodge.

Holten suddenly became aware of a wild itching above his butt. It came so unexpectedly that the scout swatted at it, imagining that some animal might be nibbling at the bandage. The itching gave way to a tingling that penetrated deep into his loins, surrounding the

59

wound. The injured area seemed to gather heat.

Thunder Woman returned with a bladder of water, a large slab of raw liver, and half a roasted buffalo hump. She dropped the fat hump meat into the pouch where the poultice had been boiled and laid out the liver on the cedar slab, then offered Eli a drink.

"Do not drink much, soon there will be a good broth for you."

"Thunder Woman," Eli blurted, excitement edging his voice. "My wound burns and tingles in a strange manner."

"Ah, Tall Bear is a strong man who possesses great medicine within. Many do not respond so quickly. I am most fortunate the wound was on your lower body, I think," she responded enigmatically, as she poured a small amount of water into a gourd drinking bowl. "I must heat your broth." She rose and began removing the cooled rocks from the pouch, preparatory to replacing them from the fire ring.

When she finished, Thunder Woman sliced the liver into narrow strips and rubbed them with salt and a pow-dered herb. She placed one end of a strip into Holten's mouth, then sliced off a bite-sized chunk when his teeth gripped it. When he had finished his meal she dipped broth from the boililng pot and after it cooled suffi-ciently, held it to his lips. All this time the hot tingle from his wound increased until it became a pulsing throb that seemed to center on the young medicine woman.

"I feel much better, Thunder Woman," Holten told the healer. "You have powerful medicine."

The bronze cheeks of the Indian darkened as she smiled, her eyes downcast.

"It is a gift I was born to, my grandmother and her

sister taught me. My grandmother said she knew I would be a great healer the day of my birth. The sky was clear, though great peals of thunder rolled across the plains.

"That is where your name came from," Holten stated. "It is very unusual."

Thunder Woman's smile faded.

"Yes," she said. "It *is* very unusual."

"Where is your husband?" Eli asked. "Is Big Wolf your man?"

The girl's firm jaw line tightened, as though she tried to hold the darkening blush that filled her face.

"If only he were," she retorted. "I would do anything to be bedded by him. As it is, all the warriors fear me. I am too powerful, and my womb aches for the swelling of a child."

"Oglala warriors do not fear a woman," the scout, who had grown into manhood during six years with the Sioux, responded coldly, surprised by his own arrogant reaction.

"Then they don't find me in their dreams," Thunder Woman said shrugging bitterly, her eyes flashing swift anger as they met Holten's for the first time. As suddenly as it happened she dropped her gaze and wiped the scout's forehead with wet deerskin, pulled the robe down to bathe his chest, then his belly, and started back up along his sides.

"Is Tall Bear feeling any pain?" she asked as Holten squirmed to better hide his trobbing erection in the folds of buffalo hide.

"A little," he lied.

"Oh?" she queried, and before he could stop her, she turned and pulled the covering off his loins to check the wound. Her jaw dropped to match the proportions of the mighty, throbbing engine that confronted her.

She covered it quickly and returned to wiping Eli's chest, then glanced up to meet his eye for the second time.

"You have — many wounds," she stammered out, then, for no apparent reason, gasped softly. Eli felt a deep, compassionate hunger gain in his heart as he realized he was going to make love to this beautiful woman. A spasm coursed his belly, leaving it tight and quivering, and melted into his chest. Was this fear that heightened his passion? Eli wondered. She did have much power. Whatever it was, the deep primordial emotion, heightened by the herbs applied to his lower body, would not be denied.

"I am a great warrior, adopted son of Two Horns, chief of forty lodges. I have been in many battles and these wounds bring me great honor."

"It is good," she whispered softly, then cleared her throat and continued. "How long do you wish to stay?"

"As soon as I can sit a horse, to pursue the man who shot me."

Thunder Woman registered surprise and disappointment.

"So soon?" she asked. "You have lost much blood, although. . ." She nearly glanced back to where the buffalo robe throbbed like a heartbeat. "Not so much as I had thought,"

Eli rose to lean on one elbow, tired of looking up at her. Sudden goose flesh prickled his skin from the rapidly chilling mountain air. Thunder Woman touched his forehead, then shook her head.

"You are going to be feverish tonight." She rose and

closed the flap of the tipi, then returned. "I think by tomorrow you will be able to ride."

Eli stared at her, unbelieving.

"There are many ways of healing," Thunder Woman began, looking at the packed earth beside Eli. "Last summer, a young boy who rode out alone to seek game, fell from his pony into a ravine. He broke many bones and we did not find him for three days. He has lost much blood from where a bone penetrated his flesh. He had not been able to eat or drink. They brought him to me. I set his bones and tended his wounds, still everyone thought he would die."

The simple honest face of the girl drew closer, her eyes glancing for only a moment up at Holten's.

"I undressed and lay next to him for most of the night, holding him to my breast as he slept in fits. My strength and healing medicine flowed into him. The next morning his flesh was whole. His uncle came and took the boy home and his bones mended quickly. He will be initiated next year. If his dreaming goes well he will become a brave."

Thunder Woman's eyes met Holten's and held defiantly.

"If Tall Bear wishes, this will work for him."

"I would find it pleasurable, even if it did not heal me." The pulse under the robe had begun to increase in tempo the instant Eli had grasped the import of her story.

The medicine woman rose and pulled her elk-skin shawl from her shoulders, then turned to one side to heft the doeskin dress over her head. Bending over she peeled off the short leggings and moccasins.

In the flickering yellow light of the fire, the sensual,

63

curved form of the girl seemed to glow from inside, as though she had a natural light within her. Absently, Thunder Woman let her hands glide slowly from her breasts, down across her rib bones, along her tight, rounded belly, down to the sybaritic flare of her hips. She slid to her knees and for a moment her hand paused above the tiny, glistening black triangle between her legs.

The medicine woman pulled the cover up and carefully slid in beside Eli, resting her head on his shoulder.

"Do you know of other ways to heal?"

For a moment she did not answer, then slowly she began, as Eli's tool thumped a steady rhythm on her belly.

"When I counted my thirteenth summer, an old medicine man, a hermit who lived high in *Khesapa*, the Black Hills, sent a messenger to my grandmother and her sister. He said he was dying, but it wasn't time yet, that he still had much to do, and he wanted them to help him live a little longer. He asked that they send me to him, and in exchange for this, he would teach me all he knew of healing."

Thunder Woman moved closer to Eli, and her large, smooth golden breasts pressed their hardened nipples into his ribs, while the soft skin of her firm belly slid across his hip.

"My grandmother told me to do everything the medicine man asked of me, and to learn well all he taught. My brother took me to where the ancient lived. When I arrived, I could tell the old man would die soon. I didn't think there was anything I could do. He took me into his tipi, he undressed me." Thunder Woman laughed and shook her head. "He studied me like a horse he'd bought. Finally he told me I was very strong, that he knew I could help him. He led me to his sleeping place, a white buffalo robe; he lay down on it, then asked me to lie next to him. He told me I was very beautiful, then touched me gently until a fire kindled in me, a fire that melted me, and I began to drip from between my legs. The old man guided my trembling limbs as he positioned me astride him."

Thunder Woman slid onto Eli's chest. He forced her to meet his eyes as she continued.

"I had never been with a man; I was afraid, afraid but eager at the same time. He told me what to do; I helped him to enter me. At first, it hurt and I wanted to stop. He held still, inside of me, and told me the pain would pass. Slowly be began to move, not enough to cause discomfort but to keep my mind on my *san*, my vagina. Soon I began to move also and looked at the old man's face. Then I knew what a good thing I was doing and could experience part of what he felt, too. Soon, like all the winds of the Earth Mother had gathered in my belly and chest, a great power surged up in me and I cried out, loud. I could have flown, but I was afraid he would not be able to stay within me."

Thunder Woman paused, pulling her eyes from Holten's impassioned gaze. She bent down and slid her lips across Eli's chest. Her breath came quickly now. Holten's raging shaft thumped against the girl's hips, teasing the fleshy shaft to even greater intensity.

"I was weak as a newborn foal the next morning," she sighed. "The medicine man was stronger than a young brave on his first warpath. There had been great *skan taku skanskan*, something in movement, spiritual vitalilty between us. I stayed with him for three moons and and cried when he sent me home. He told me to practice what I had learned."

The medicine girl raised her shapely rear, letting the stout and throbbing shaft ease between her legs and into her waiting hand.

"He taught me many other things as well," the little healer continued, "but these are the ones I wanted to tell you about."

With skilled hands she worked her pink petals until they parted, moist and hot. Then she took the powerful, spasming lance against and between them.

Eli groaned mightily as he entered the tight opening to her body that wrapped hungrily around his shaft. A moment of delirious excitement coursed through the impaled healer, excitement that Eli could feel heaped upon his own, and he nearly fainted from the excess. Her hips began a slow undulation, with the smooth rhythm of a swimming trout, then settled down to a grinding, rocking motion.

Eli's pulsating cock ached and stretched at its skin while his breath came quick and deep, and he knew that if he were on top he'd lose control. Thunder Woman licked at Eli's nipple as she worked the head of the scout's penis ever deeper into her healing cavern until it throbbed at the very entrance to her womb. Slippery hot, her muscular passage seemed to suck at the intruder, pulling him deeper in, until she was sitting down hard on the massive weapon.

She began a rocking dance on the pole, sliding up the full length until it started to slip out and at the last moment popping it back through her opening and falling to plunge it deep within her, the magic juices running warm, tickling paths down Eli's balls.

She drew her shoulders back, thrusting her pert, high

breasts with their long nipples and full areolas into the air. Eli took them into his hands and began to knead those matchless orbs.

"Do not let yourself go," she cried through animal grunts and whimpers. "The longer you last, the more power you gain."

"How convenient," Eli grunted through his efforts to contain himself. In an attempt to hold out he took his weather-roughened hands from those delicious breasts and made the mistake of running them down her sides. The effect was so nearly disastrous he redoubled his determination. Suddenly he knew he was in complete control and he felt the flow of energy that came from the fabulous body that writhed in ecstasy upon him. He stretched and groaned like a young bear, regretting the wound that prevented him from matching her healing efforts.

She climaxed suddenly, with a sharp loud wail that must have waked the whole camp. She struggled wildly on Eli's shaft, like a feral filly at breaking time. A half-scream, half-groan rent the quiet mountain air. Her face looked heavenward and contorted into an animal death mask.

She collapsed to Eli's chest, exhaustion racing her breath, but her bucking hips only slowed.

"You feel stronger," she whispered.

"Yes," he answered. "Much stronger."

By morning, after many long hours of enthusiastic healing, Eli felt like a buffalo bull roaming across the soft expanses of Thunder Woman's moist prairie. A moment before dawn, after a solid hour's sleep, Eli crawled onto the healer's chest. Her hot lips fell desperately along the nape of his neck as he brought his weapon to a powerful stance, then buried it between the still lubricated walls of the inviting passage. He spent another long healing session with Thunder Woman, until he felt a flaming liquid river build against the base of his spine.

Tingling and itching, it surged and pressed until, with a mighty roar, Holten dumped the entire flood into the delicate chamber between his healer's legs.

Thunder Woman leapt with the power of his climax and bucked into her own.

They lay there locked together, motionless, for a long time. Finally, with a sigh of regret, Thunder Woman rocked her hips, and Eli's woman-slicked organ plopped against the foundation robe of their bower.

"We have shared a powerful medicine, Tall Bear," the woman whispered with a sigh. "How is your wound?" The question was accompanied by a gesture to roll over, so Eli presented his injured posterior for examination. Thunder Woman removed the bandages, then the boiled moss poultice.

"You are *iktomi*, grizzly bear, the wound heals much already. I will sew it closed, but first we heat broth, for I must boil a hair from the horse's tail." The medicine woman covered Eli against the early morning chill, except for his head and rump, then proceeded with her chorers while he dozed.

Eli woke to the delicious aroma of hump stew and a warm hand on his rear.

"This will hurt a little *misinksi*, my heart. At least you will not have to submit to an awl and bone needle. These fine tools have been in my family since my grandmother was a little girl." The healer displayed a sailmaker's curved needle and rusty pliers that must have dated from pre-steam days on the Missouri River. Eli stifled a groan and tried to smile his appreciation; it beat the hell out of the alternative. Surreptitiously he filched a cartridge from his belt and bit down hard on the exposed bullet when the medicine woman went to work.

Eli's wound was duly stitched, a fresh poultice applied and bandaged in place. He'd drunk his broth and done considerable damage to the sweet, fat-laced hump meat. At the moment he wasn't even mad at Bart Blackwell because the magic herbs of the healer were sending waves of heat through his loins, and he was deeply engrossed in the compound curves of Thunder Woman's rear as she leaned over the cooking pouch.

Suddenly all hell broke loose outside Holten's sanctuary. Trouble?

Chapter Six

The noise outside became more urgent as Eli pulled on his pants. He was amazed at how much better he felt. Aside from the pesky tingle, there was some tightness from the stitches, and of course some loose front teeth from the ruined .44-40 slug. He snatched his Remington from where Big Wolf had laid it across his saddle and pushed the entrance flap upward. From there he saw what the ruction was all about.

"I am a man of God, I mean your people no harm." Reverend Smith stood before Big Wolf, who stoically studied the man in black.

The minister eased toward his mount, although a brave held the reins, as well as a rusty Sharps Carbine on the holy man.

"I saw the smoke and thought I'd come over." Smith eased his hat off and smiled nervously. He started toward the pack mule he led, only to run into another rifle barrel.

"If I'm intruding, why I'll just — move on."

"No hurry, Reverend. Stay for breakfast."

Smith saw the scout and relief flooded his face.

"Halleluiah!" he shouted. "I thought I *was* breakfast!"

Quickly, Eli explained to Big Wolf who Smith was.

"This one friend to you?" the war chief pressed, not satisfied with Holten's merely knowing the camp intruder.

"Yes," the scout said and nodded. "The preacher is my friend."

"Do you speak their language, Mr. Holten?" Smith asked.

"Call me Eli, Reverend."

"Then you'll have to call me Zeke." The preacher beamed.

"I lived with the Sioux for six years," the scout explained. "Where's the rest of the posse?"

Sadly, Zeke raised his hands, then let them fall to his sides.

"You're lookin' at it," he announced.

Eli's jaw muscles bulged. He studied the preacher's face carefully.

"I started out with ten 'good men and true'," Smith began to explain. "After the first day, half of them had to go back to tend their business. By the second day, the rest didn't want to miss the hangin'."

"There ain't goin' to be any hanging until we round up this Blackwell hombre," Holten pointed out.

"The circuit judge rode in whilst we were packing up to follow you, Eli," Zeke countered. "He wants to try an' hang Matthew Blackwell at the earliest possible." The holy man sighed. "Besides, some of the good citizens of Eagle Butte didn't like being in a posse headed up by a man o' God. It seems to lack a certain sense of brag value."

"Come, sit my lodge, eat. Tell Big Wolf why chase white man, why him shoot Tall Bear."

Ain't that enough reason, Eli thought. He grunted acceptance and went back to the lodge to retrieve a shirt and his bowl. "Waugh!" A full belly and good manners

71

required him to eat hearty, no excuses.

"I'm going to unsaddle my animals," the preacher stated.

"Thunder Woman, where's my Winchester?" Holten inquired.

"I took it to the lodge of my aunt for cleaning. Leave the revolver and I will clean it. Your rifle will be here before you need it."

"Whatever I do, you do," Holten admonished the preacher.

They entered the dwelling of the war chief. Eli circled the fire pit to the right and seated himself in the place of an honored guest, to the chief's left. The minister carefully copied the scout's action and sat down next to him. Two women entered, collected their bowls and exited for the cookfires outside.

Big Wolf brought out the pipe. He ceremoniously loaded the bowl of the feather-decorated, sacred smoking implement. Then he made offering to the six directions, East, West, North, South, to the Sky above and the Earth Mother below. The Oglala chief lit the smoking mixture with care, sucked at the stem until the contents glowed bright red. Creamy tendrils floated to the tipi's smoke flaps. Big Wolf offered the calumet to the scout.

With practiced ease, Eli repeated the ritual of the pipe, lifting it to the six directions, then sucked at its stem until it glowed once again.

He offered the pipe to the Reverend. Eli hoped he would be able to enlist the aid of Big Wolf. The offer of hospitality was a good sign.

Zeke Smith copied the ceremony, down to the grim look on his face. He puffed billowy smoke from his mouth, then looked to Eli for a reaction.

Holten winked and the preacher passed the pipe on around the circle of warriors who had followed them into the lodge. When Big Wolf had smoked again he rose, holding the pipe, and spoke in the Lakota language. Another good omen as it signified the talk would bear on matters that could be of importance to entire village.

"It is a good thing, Tall Bear. Tell us why you are here, why you pursue this person and the reason he shot you." He handed the pipe to his guest.

Eli told the whole story, the bank robbery and killing, even tried to explain Zeke's position. The closest he could come to that one was to compare his status to that of a medicine man on the warpath.

"I don't like the white man's black robes. What you say of this one sounds like he is a good man. Does he read the omens well?"

Eli employed skillful invention.

"Has this medicine man counted many coups?"

Eli lied with imagination and flair while the poor Reverend looked on bewildered, knowing he was the subject of Holten's dramatic monologue but understanding not a word.

"This person has wrestled with the demons that come out of the dark place below the earth and won the contest. This medicine chief of the whites has many times brought cooling, healing rains by his prayers. He has recently, and I witnessed it, disarmed a dangerous renegade, who held a gun to his head. For this he used the power of the black book he carries." That last was true enough, Eli thought. And it did constitute counting

73

coup. "He fights with the strength of many and is here alone because the faint of heart would not go where he leads."

The warriors grunted their awe and gazed with new respect at the holy man.

The scout wound up a chest-thumping passage on Zeke's virtues, then finished his story with an account of his pursuit of Blackwell and the desperado's bushwhack.

"What will Tall Bear do now?" Big Wolf queried.

"I feel good this morning," Eli boasted. "I will pursue this person and either capture him, or leave him for the wolves to eat. That will be up to him."

Big Wolf shook his head.

"Thunder Woman's medicine is more powerful than I thought," the warrior sighed, a knowing twinkle in his eyes. "You were so weak, I felt shame for you. Now I see a strong warrior, ready to do battle." The chief looked amused. "It was very loud healing." He grinned gleefully. "She cried out many times last night. I think she find man pretty soon now."

Eli remembered what the healer had said about wanting to bed the warrior chief and he smiled.

"She is very powerful. All her medicine is good and she will bring great honor to a man." Holten thought a moment. "Think of the power and courage her sons would have. They would be as *Mahto*, the grizzly bear. That is," Holten motioned loosely with his hands, as if dismissing the thought, "if they were sired by a truly great warrior."

Big Wolf nodded, the slightest seed of a thought planted in his agile but innocent mind.

"I have always thought of her as a healer, not a woman."

"A *young* woman," Eli amended.

"Do you wish help in catching this person?" Big Wolf asked bluntly.

The scout thought a moment. A plan had been fermenting in his mind. Now he asked for what he thought he'd need.

"Five horses," Eli said. "Five fresh animals that I shall return to you."

"Do you plan to trample this person in a stampede?" Big Wolf laughed heartily at his joke and the others readily joined him.

"No, just run him to ground."

The women served food: trout, caught in a nearby stream, steamed cattail bulbs, and wild berries, followed by the inevitable buffalo, this time in the form of roast hump ribs. In spite of misgivings, the scout acquitted himself admirably until Thunder Woman showed up with her cedar slab covered with thin strips of raw liver, salted and sprinkled with ground herbs.

"You must eat this," she instructed. "It will replace the blood you lost." Then she turned and left him to the task.

Eli had eaten till he doubted his ability to stand. Right now the liver did not look the least palatable. Yet, as Eli knew, Indians who did not follow a healer's instructions to the letter often died, usually about the time a white doctor would have declared the cure complete. Somehow, he got the liver down while wondering if he'd done Big Wolf any favor. The latter puffed the pipe and watched him.

"You shall have the horses," Big Wolf agreed. "Some of my warriors have gone to track the white man who shot you. They are leaving a trail for you to follow."

I hope they don't catch him, Holten reflected privately. I wish that pleasure.

"One of the scouts returned before dawn. They have instructions not to be seen. Who knows? One of them is very young. He may count *coup* if his blood gets too hot. You may pick up the trail where Bent Creek flows into the Netawaka."

Eli returned to Thunder Woman's lodge to retrieve his plunder. The young healer waited for him.

"I am very tired, *Mihigna.*" She answered when the scout asked how she felt. "It is the nature of this medicine to draw from one and give to the other if it is desired. It can strengthen either, or both. Also it has the same power to weaken. You must let me freshen your bandage."

"Uh . . . Thunder Woman, I . . . uh, oh, shit. I can't be your husband. I work for the American horse soldiers. No way I can make meat for a family. No way!"

"No matter. I was alone before you came, I will be alone when you are gone, until your son comes. No one need make kills for me. My arts assure meat whenever I travel. Everything I need is guaranteed. You are *mihigna.*"

Eli had turned and jerked his shirt up and was unbuckling his belt as she spoke. He wisely held his peace.

Thunder Woman pulled his pants down and reached around to untie the bandage.

"What do you mean?" he blurted. "Son?"

"Oh yes," she cooed. "These things I know about."

"Shit!"

"It is a good thing," she said, sounding hurt. "No other man will sleep in my lodge. Now I will have a son to teach my medicine. He will become the most famous healer on the plains. Besides, I know other medicine,

76

too." The last carried a hint of threat. The medicine woman slapped a fresh, very hot poultice on the wound and tied it in place as Eli tried to keep from dancing.

"There, this time when the medicine begins to work maybe you cool your lance in a coyote, eh?" She glided through the flap and out of sight.

The tingling and itching began to build, even as Eli strapped on his Remington.

Big Wolf rode up to the lodge with a string of fine ponies as Zeke finished off saddling his jaded animals. A young brave led Sonny to Eli as he carried his tack from the tent. The young warrior's countenance looked grave and he motioned to the bullet graze across Sonny's upper flank. It was festering.

Eli turned back into the tipi and recovered the used poultice. This he carried to his stallion and squeezed several drops into the injury.

"I was countin' on you to finish this show on, old boy. Looks like your stayin', though. Damn, the next generation o' ponies around here will all be half Morgan when this stuff starts working."

"Five of my best ponies," the war chief bragged as soon as he had Eli's attention. "They will help you to catch that bad person."

"You are a true friend, Big Wolf," Eli stated as Zeke began to transfer his gear to the new animals. Before the chief could start to enumerate the virtues of each beast, Eli spoke again. "To show my appreciation, I'll leave this fine stallion until I return your ponies. He'll breed some brave stock for you." Sonny trumpeted agreement, then turned to sniff at the strange sensation that spread outward from his wound.

"Ride swiftly, bring honor to yourself and my ponies.

I wait for your return and to hear of your *coups*."

Outside Eagle Butte's Thunder Saloon and Hotel, the temperature dipped with every blast of the chilling North Wind. Inside, however, sheer body heat and cigar smoke kept the ladies on the balcony of the second story briskly waving fans in their faces.

Circuit Court Judge, Louis B. Thornton, sat behind the circular gambling table that doubled as a makeshift court bench. He licked his lips and grinned through his jowls up at Allison, who smiled behind her fan and flirted unashamedly with His Honor. His Honor flirted unashamedly right back.

The twelve jurors filed in from behind the bar, taking their seats to the right of the defendant. The foreman remained standing, then coughed loudly to get the distracted jurist's attention. Thornton jumped when the sweating marshal, who looked as ill as he felt, dropped the butt of his rifle on the floor with a loud bang.

"Come to order, come to order!" The judge cried, rapping the table with his gavel. His loose, fleshy form jiggled with each blow. Thornton turned somberly to the standing juror.

"Mr. Foreman," the judge intoned. "Have you reached a verdict?"

"Yes, sir, er . . . Yer Honor, we have, Yer Honor," the foreman answered up. "We find the defendant so damn guilty we all can't wait ta spit on his grave."

The packed barroom reverberated with cheers.

Judge Thornton punished the table top with his gavel, tearing his eyes from little Allison who was sliding her hands rhythmically between her legs.

"Order, order I say!" His forehead glistened and there was a husky tremble in his voice. "Is there a recommendation for clemency?"

"Hell, no, Yer Honor." The foreman was the counter clerk and teller from the robbed bank. "Wouldn't do no good ta spit on an empty grave."

"Does the defendant have anything to say before I pass sentence?"

"Bet your *ass* I do!" Matthew Blackwell screamed as he leapt to his feet. He spun on his young attorney. "Y're mah lawyer . . . *object!* Y've seen this farce. Ah want a change o' . . . a change o' . . . another trial somewheres else."

The defense attorney sighed and came to his feet.

"If I may address the bench, Your Honor," he listlessly began. "The defense would like you to declare a mistrial and change of venue."

"On what grounds?"

"Well—Good God, Your Honor," the attorney answered, flustered. He pointed at the jury. "Every single man on the jury saw the crime committed! They only stopped work on the gallows long enough for the trial."

"I should think this would please the defense," the judge stated. "That's twelve fewer witnesses to take the stand against your client."

The defense opened his mouth, hesitated, then chuckled. "Hey, Lou, that's rich. No wonder you're a judge."

"The court finds you guilty of murder in the first degree," the bench decreed, while Thornton's eyes drifted back up to Allison, who now leaned over the rail to expose her ample cleavage. "It sentences you to death by

79

hanging. The marshal, at his convenience, shall take you from this place to that normally reserved for execution and there shall hang you by the neck, until you are dead, dead, dead." The judge turned his eyes to meet with Blackwell's and pronounced the benediction. "In your case may the Lord forget he knows you." His gaze snapped back to Allison. "This court is adjourned! I have a —" The judge looked up to see Allison hitch her skirt up and rock her luscious torso invitingly. "— a pressing engagement—that cannot wait."

They had come a long way, in far less time than he had anticipated. Nathan Barlow felt considerable satisfaction. Even allowing for their southward diversion, they had crossed Kansas and the riverboat had taken them speedily into Nebraska. A long ride after leaving the *Selkirk* at North Platte and only the previous evening the gang made camp in Dakota Territory. Concern that they might be recognized prevented a faster route by staying aboard to Pierre. Less than two hundred miles separated them from Eagle Butte. Soon . . . soon now, revenge would be tasting sweet on his lips.

"Rider comin' this way," John Hay informed Nathan as the young outlaw rode back from his position on the point. "Ridin' like all the demons o' Hell are on his tail."

The senior Barlow detached himself from the other men and rode forward with his scout. They stopped short of a low rise and dismounted. Nathan took a pair of stolen field glassed from his saddle bags and crawled to the top of the ridge.

Nathan Barlow looked through his binoculars at the

prairie that spread out ahead of them. Like John Hay had told him, a foam-flecked horse stumbled across the open grass, its hatless rider brutally slashing the animal's flanks.

"A man that treats his hoss thata way, oughta be shot," Nathan growled, scratching under his capote. The men had changed to work clothes shortly after their disembarkation from the river boat at Pierre.

"We gonna find out what's goin' on?" Hay asked.

"Best that we do," Nathan replied. He turned to John and smiled at his new friend. At a signal from Nathan, the fifteen killers began to amble down toward the rider.

Bart Blackwell gulped in air. It burned at his parched tongue, even as he gasped it out again. The lathered mare he rode shuddered with exhaustion, then missed her footing and crashed to the ground with a blood-chilling scream. Bart catapulted over the animal's head and sprang to his feet, panic in every move. He ran back and kicked the hapless horse to her feet. She stood, spraddle-legged, her head down and coughing bloody froth between efforts to breathe. An exhausted, self-pitying, whine escaped the young derelict, helplessness and fear overcoming him.

It had been a week, and for all that time, the man he had ambushed pursued him, though he had run in circles and exhausted every trick he knew. "Ah knowed Ah should'a finished that bastard off when Ah had the chanst'," Bart wailed aloud. He hadn't though. His burning eyes glared at the ground, now with a dying horse. The hunter would soon be upon him. Blackwell scrubbed his tearing eyes with the grubby sleeve of his shirt.

Shadows fell on his blurred vision. Startled, he screamed his childish, terrorized rage and reeled against the oblivious mare.

Fifteen huge, threatening shadows resolved into men on horses as his eyes cleared. Hard, grim-faced men. A posse? There was no tree to hang him from. They'd surely have to shoot him dead. Good. God, don't let them hang him.

"Allright! Do it!" he shrieked. "Ah don't care no more. Go ahead, get it over with. I didn't wanna rob your silly bank no way." A sudden thought squirmed through the despairing panic. "It was Matthew, he made me! It warn't my fault."

The older rider, who seemed like the leader to Bart, looked quizzically at the man next to him, then back at the sweating boy who cowered against his dying mare.

"*You* robbed a bank?" Nate asked.

"You ain't the Eagle Butte posse?" Bart blurted.

"We sure ain't no posse," Harlan Bowes said with a snicker.

"*You* held up the bank at the Mercantile Store in Eagle Butte?" Jed asked incredulously, pronouncing each word in stunned deliberation. Then he smirked. "Beat us to it, did ja?"

Blackwell straightened up. He licked his lips, then hope burst into his heart. He smiled experimentally.

With swift precision, Nate drew his big Remington and fired. Blackwell flopped on the ground and a neat blue hole appeared, halfway between ear and eye level and smack in the center of the mare's forehead. Thick black blood erupted from her nostrils, her knees buckling, and she dropped straight down. The body would have rolled over but Bart's shivering form blocked it, pinning him to the ground.

"Jumpy, ain't ya boy?" Nate growled from his dancing mount. "Hay, get down there and jerk that piece a shit loose."

"Now, boy," Nate continued, when Blackwell was on his feet again. "What's this about a posse from Eagle Butte? Is Marshal Peters with it?"

"Don't know about a posse," Bart whined. "There's a man named Eli Holten chasin' me an' he ain't rightly human." His eyes sought the horizon without conscious volition. "Nearly caught up to me this mornin'."

Jed's jaw dropped. Slowly a grin grew on Nate's face until it stretched from both ears and exposed yellow, horse teeth.

"Damn," he whispered. "Damn!"

"You know him?" Bart asked apprehensively.

"Sure do. The Lord's will is bein' done. My name is Nate Barlow and I plan ta kill him."

Once again, hope surged in the scrawny breast of Bart Blackwell, then awe. His eyes swept over the lean, tough men of the Barlow Gang and he knew he was saved.

"Ah'm Bart Blackwell," he said, reaching out to shake the hand of his savior. "Ah'll take yuh back ta where he was this mornin'."

"Double up with John Hay there," growled Nate, irritated at having to ride with such low-life scum.

"What about my saddle?"

"Leave it," Nate grunted. Then, "Split your saddle bags and soogan among the boys. Let's ride."

The outlaws lined out to the northwest under

Bart's direction.

"You get away with any loot from Eagle Butte?" John queried.

"We tried," he started, his smile faded. "That damned marshal bushwhacked us."

"Bushwhacked ya, huh?" Nate snorted.

"Jumped 'em while they was goin' about their lawful business, no doubt," Art Hawkins said. Nate shot him a baleful glance.

"Strikes me Holten probably rode all night ta come up on ya this mornin'," Nate ventured. "He'll still be trailin' one man an' prob'ly stop to sleep some. You ride near Stone Holler?"

"Yuh mean that big rock pile that's jest over the rise?" Bart asked eagerly. "I climbed up there tuh check muh back trail."

"Yep," Nate concurred. "They's flat ground down in the center, 's where the name come from. We'll just hole up around the rim of that basin and when he shows up, we'll blast Mr. Scout, Eli Holten, into the hottest corner of Hell."

Chapter Seven

A courier from Fort Pierre rode into the lone street of Eagle Butte. His first stop was at the Thunder Saloon for a beer. It'd been a long ride.

The cavalryman swallowed the cool draught of bitters in one breath, wiped his face with the back of his hand and looked around the saloon.

"I got a message for the marshal," the soldier announced to the room in general as he produced a moist sheet of paper from his pouch. "Can someone direct me to his office?"

From the second story balcony that hung over the bar, jowly chuckles and an angelic tittering burst from a door that swung open to let the rotund form of Judge Louis B. Thornton, with his arm around the shoulders of the heavenly Allison, stumble to the railing.

"But I must be off!" The eminent jurist's rolling tone drew every eye.

"You've been goin' off since you hit town," Allison giggled from behing a tiny hand.

"No. No my dear," His Honor chortled. "I mean I must ride to Lantry, in furtherance of the cause of justice for this beknighted land!"

"Can't you stay till Eli Holten gets back?" asked the lightly rouged dove with a serious demeanor.

"It would be my pleasure to meet that fine gentleman

of the plains again, Chickadee," Thornton responded. "He would understand that I have already taried too long. There are criminals to be tried, murderers to be hanged, rustlers to be incarcerated!"

The judge turned to the few midday customers who loitered about the saloon.

"*So,* good day to *all* you fine people! Is there anything else that I, Judge Louis B. Thornton, can do in the service of this *fine* community!"

"Yes, sir," the cavalryman suggested. "Ya could tell me where I might find the marshal?"

Marshal Orsen Peters lay in bed, squirming with the pain of his infected shoulder that had caused him to sweat and chill all day. His daughter Amy cooled his forehead with a wet towel in one hand as she wiped away yellow-green pus with the other.

The courier squirmed, too, at the sight of the putrid wound. He gave the message to Amy Peters, glanced again at the injured lawman and bolted from the room. certain he had detected the smell of rotten flesh.

"What's it say?" Peters asked.

"It is from the commandant at Fort Leavenworth, Daddy. It says part of the Barlow Gang was lynched near Eudora, Kansas. Oh Daddy, it says they have evidence the Barlows are bound for Coffeville. You needn't worry about them for a while."

"If the army knows where that bunch is headed, it won't be long before no one worries about them," the marshal speculated.

Amy sat on her father's bed, concern in her fine

brown eyes.

"Should I tell the town, Daddy?" Amy asked. "They'd be awfully relieved."

"You c'n tell 'em, Honey, but I sure's hell don't plan to relax till them Kansans got 'em all hung."

Eli rode hard, as he'd done for the last seven days and all of the previous night. There'd been a two hour nap this morning after locating Blackwell's deserted camp. Eli'd hoped to get ahead of the fugitive with that all night ride, or at least catch in him in his soogans. He had no idea how close he had come. Bart had actually seen Eli coming and run for his life. Unfortunately it was on a hardpacked trail that showed none of the usual signs of recent passage.

The scout felt a jerk and looked back. The rearmost of the two spare ponies had shied again, a habit that caused Eli to tie him Indian fashion to the tail of the more trailwise pony he led. Damn, he'd probably have saved time by listening to Big Wolf's lecture on his fine animals. At least he could have figured from omission of various virtures which ones had faults instead of learning it on the trail.

Holten figured the next time he rode that particular beast it would have no time to look for something to get spooked over. At any rate, the fugitive could not be far ahead. This day would see the death of Bart's horse; Eli was as sure of that as he was of the fact that Blackwell's animal was a gallant little buckskin mare. They never puddled piss the way a stud or gelding did, and she'd left hair where she scratched on a tree.

Eli wondered how far behind Zeke Smith had lagged. He didn't plan another one-on-one fight. Pin the bastard down and wait for the odd preacher to come up and provide the distraction. Then it'd be simple.

Up ahead, a pile of boulders came abruptly into view as Eli topped a slight swell. A perfect ambush spot. He had no cover and the kid had a rifle that ranged his Winchester. Eli stood in the stirrups, easing his damaged butt. The wound had knit unbelievably fast. Eli had cut and pulled the horsehair stitches four days back. What a chore that had been.

As Eli stared at the huge rock pile he suddenly discerned the figure of a man moving across the face of a white granite slab. Yup, the son-of-a-bitch stood out like a nun in a whorehouse. The scout dismounted to lower his profile and retreated about a hundred yards to a dry buffalo wallow he'd cataloged. His buttocks itched and he wished he could get some more of Thunder Woman's special brand of healing.

Eli hobbled his horses and removed the saddle from the one he had been riding. Then carried his saddle bags to the rim of the depression. He dug out his field glasses, made a tent of the leather bags to shade the lens, and began to study Stone Hollow.

The sun headed for its daily death in the west, lighting all the brilliant panoply of color that attended this ceremony on the Great Plains. Purple shadow fled from the stone promontory on his right as the rock to his left faded from brilliant pink to rose red. Still, nothing more had moved.

The scout retrieved his gear and dropped back into the wallow with his horses and chewed jerky from his saddle bags, as he rationed water from a large skin, carried by one of the spare ponies. Next, Eli settled down for a nap.

An icy wind whistled and moaned eerily through the rocks Nathan Barlow had chosen for an ambush. Bart Blackwell felt the chill right down in his soul. What kind of camp didn't have no fire? Blackwell thought bleakly. A fugitives' camp. The sort of dreary resting place he'd made for the last week. Christ! At sixteen to one he figured they ought to ride the bastard down.

Bart didn't dare to complain out loud as he sat there pitying his lot. The outlaw leader wanted a cold camp to help them catch Holten, and Blackwell didn't intend to give him a bad time about that. Besides, Bart didn't think Barlow would take much shit from anyone. The young derelict sat huddled in his blanket, watching the other men cleaning their weapons and otherwise preparing for the kill.

Nate Barlow studied the newly acquired member of his gang in disgust.

"You can never get away from 'em huh, Jed?" He motioned to Blackwell.

"It's jus' somethin' ya have ta live with Nate," Jed philosophized. Then he worried off another bite of jerky.

Bart noticed the other men staring at him and he smiled like an orphan puppy, exposing rotten teeth. Both Barlows turned away in disgust.

Nathan Barlow's thoughts ranged back over the years and he spoke in a quiet whisper to his brother. "Remember back when we was kids? How Momma and Poppa would take us to the camp meetin's? Oh, how the choir would sing and praise the Lord. Always made me git a lump in my throat. I could pray and shout as long and loud as any of them. An' the preachin'. . . . ah, how those circuit riders could fill the air with fire and brimstone. Scairt the bejezus outta me.

" 'Member when Paw caught me playin' with m'self. Couldn't been over eight or so. He made me go up front at the next tent revival and give myself to Jesus. 'Fore we runned away from home, I got born again five times."

"Didn't do much good, you axs me," Jed scoffed. "You turned owlhoot all the same."

"I'm doin' what I have to," Nathan protested. "An' I fear the Lord and listen to Him. It's Him tells me what must be done."

"Like killin' that marshal an' Eli Holten?"

"Sure's there's a hope of Heaven." His eyes narrowed. "An' anybody else who gits in my way."

Eli woke with a start, then lay still, staring at the stars where they wheeled among the wind-tattered, moonlit clouds. He sighed with relief. It was only around ten o'clock, plenty of time for what he had in mind. Reaching into his bedroll he extracted a pair of finely beaded moccasins and slid out of his boots and socks. He wriggled his toes, enjoying the icy cold for a moment, then put on the more supple footgear.

He checked his Remington for dirt that might have worked into the action and felt along his cartridge belt to be sure none had fallen out. His hand brushed reassuringly against the shaft of his sheathed Bowie as he scrambled from the hole.

The clouds racing across the sky created periods when the night seemed pitch black compared to the glare from the three quarter moon. On these occasions the scout made good time toward the ominous pile of boulders. When the moon poured her silvery light on the grass, Eli crawled only as the wind moved the grass, taking no chances, until he reached the edge of the rocks.

On silent feet, Eli started up and over the maze. He felt out each step before he took it. He gained a vantage point that offered some cover. The obscuring clouds worked against him now. He saw many things that appeared to move, even though he did not look directly at them, and knew what poor light did to the imagination. He could not identify one of these shadows as Blackwell. Impatiently he waited for more light.

A long thin cloud passed its last tendril across the moon. Silver light flooded the basin in the center of Stone Hollow.

Suddenly Eli realized that all the things he had seen that could have been the fugitive *were* people, armed and waiting men. They could only be waiting for him.

There was one thing to do: get the hell out of there and lay low until daylight to reconnoiter. Who the hell were they? Only a band of desperados like the Barlow Gang could muster so many men. Who else would protect a fugitive with an ambush? If it were Barlow, he had to have covered a great deal of distance in a relatively short time. His only reason for being here would be to take revenge on Eagle Butte. The town must be warned. He could gather up Zeke on his way north.

The scout began to pick a route back toward his horses. Suddenly a loud crack, close to Holten's ears,

91

ended any chance of escaping undetected. The bullet spattered his head with stone and lead fragments. Eli returned fire, his Remington leaping into his hand to roar defiance at a fading muzzle bloom that still had shape only in the mind's eye. A loud, startled grunt announced Eli had done rather well. Quickly now, he broke toward the grass, bearing east toward a creek bed in an attempt to lead them away from his horses.

Somewhere below, a big rifle flared, rolling deafening thunder around the basin of rock. Voices cried out to his right and in front, and Eli bent his course more to the left.

"Someone was up in them rocks," a voice bellowed. Its familiarity chilled the soul of Eli Holten. It bore the unmistakable stamp of Nathan Barlow.

"I'm hit," another voice whimpered.

"Don't shoot unless ya see him," Nathan roared. "If ya hear a shot, work toward it."

Now things got a little tougher, Eli thought. Fire a shot and he'd let the bastards know where he was.

The sudden turn of events still had Holten struggling to think. He'd been after one stupid but sneaky desperado. Now he had encountered a nest full and he had to run for his life. Desperate cunning raced through the scout's mind. His six years of living with the Oglala Sioux and their combat wisdom directed his actions. He pulled his Bowie knife as the moon ducked behind another cloud.

The clatter of boots on the rock rang loud to the hunted man. There was a regular crowd out there.

Cautiously, the scout worked his way through the boulders and around the camp nestled in the center of them. If the darkness held, there was a slim chance to sneak past the Barlow Gang and reach the open prairie. He edged quickly around the huge chunks of granite, keeping the camp to his left. He wanted to move out of the rocks and across the hollow which was the most direct route he could see. He nearly made it undetected.

Again the clouds proved an ally. Holten stepped into shadow in the split second the newly exposed moon created it. Illuminated by the sudden light, a man's hat faced Eli, not ten feet away.

"That you Hay?" the outlaw spoke softly.

"Yup, seen anything?" Eli replied in the same muted tone.

"Huh, last Ah seed was the muzzle flash on the other side when he shot Jed." As he spoke, the hat turned and an arm that terminated in a revolver gestured across the basin.

Eli leapt, taking the man from beside and a little behind. One hand covered the gunman's mouth while the other punched the Bowie up under his victim's sternum, then through the heart.

The struggle was brief. Hot blood drenched the scout's hand and arm nearly to the elbow as it gushed around the tightly held knife. A nicked lung made a noise like a wet fart in Sunday School while thrashing feet scraped wildly at the hollow's floor of decomposed granite. Eli bent over backwards to lift the dead man's feet, and his shins took a wild, if short spurring. When movement faded to involuntary shudders and occasional convulsions, Eli eased the corpse to the ground, surprised as always the racket had not been heard.

The scout jerked the former outlaw's shirt tail out and wiped his knife and hand thoroughly while listening for any belated alarm. The darkness had become his element, something he understood and his opponents did not.

Eli's first objective was the stream. If he could reach it, it would be a simple matter to circle around to his horses, then ride north along his own back trail to pick up the reverend and warn Eagle Butte. There was little doubt he could beat the Barlow Gang to the town with his relay of ponies.

Once into the grass, Eli set off at a trot, keeping a wary eye on the thickening clouds. Holten sensed, rather than saw, a sudden darkening of the earth that paralleled his path. At the instant of revelation, the ground underfoot sagged, then fell away with a dull thump. The wash, all of a four foot drop, might have been a dangerously deep one for all Holten knew, and his efforts to save himself did not ease his fall. The right ankle twisted hard.

The scout suppressed a yelp of agonized surprise, falling clear of the soft slide onto the hard bottom of the gully. For a moment he sat quietly, working to draw air into tortured lungs, then tried to rise. The moment he put weight on his right leg, it collapsed.

Nathan Barlow lit another lucifer and studied the dead shootist that lay in the rocks.

"I figured he snuck around," Barlow told Jed and Tony, then pointed to the open prairie as a strong gust of north wind blew the match out. "He went that way."

Jed held a bloody cloth against his shoulder wound.

"It was Eli Holten, Nate." The wounded brother gasped. "I'd know that face, even lit by the powder he shot me with."

"He'll pay, brother," Nate promised. "The Good Book says 'vengenace is mine.' "

"Don't that read, 'vengeance is mine, sayeth the Lord'?" blurted Tony. Even in the dark, the hired gun felt Barlow's burning eyes bake his face.

"Well, I—I don't know my Bible all that well anyway," he hastily apologized.

In groups of two, the Barlow Gang began to zigzag to the southeast through the dark, moonlit prairie.

Holten inspected the ankle as he sat with his back to one wall of the gully. The scout's greatest fear was that he may have broken the bone. If so he'd have no way of moving quickly enough to get away from Barlow. He'd never make it to his horses before dawn, and by the light of day the large band of rustlers and cutthroats would find him. Eli felt the ankle and wriggled it gently. Already it had begun to swell, and Eli knew better than to believe the axiom that "if you can move it, it ain't broke." Like most things "everybody knows," *it just ain't so,* was more his style.

Abruptly the noise of boots thrashing through dry grass surrounded the scout. Holten hugged the shadow of the bank, for the moon had broken through again. The whole Barlow Gang had gotten on the move, hunting him. As quickly as the moonlight had come, it disappeared, making the night darker for its brief effort.

There came a terrified scream.

"Damn! I'm hurt!" It was the voice of Bart Blackwell.

"What happened?" Nathan yelled. Someone else

stumbled and fell in.

"Shit," the man yelled. "There's a washout here, 's all hidden in the grass. Be keerful or someone'll get a broke laig."

"We cain't find nothin' like this. Holten coulda been down there and knifed another man or two," Tony confided to his boss. Barlow didn't answer for a moment as he studied the wind that blew, cold and hard from the north.

"Call the boys back to the rocks," Nathan decided. "We'll let Gawd do our killin' fer us."

The thrashing of feet started back the way they had come and soon disappeared altogether. The scout knew he had to move. The noise of his enemy's retreat gave him a chance to escape. Eli rose again, keeping his weight on his left foot, against the bank. Downstream would lead to the creek, then upstream to the northwest side of Stone Hollow. Then perhaps five hundred yards to the buffalo wallow and his ponies. Granted enough time and a little luck, it was possible.

The gang members followed their leader's instruction and constructed torches, twisted from dry grass, as Cooper lit a sheltered fire just within the ring of boulders.

"Gawd said, 'let there be light,' " Nathan intoned. "Then again, 'ask, and ye shall receive.' Ah'm askin' fer the life a Eli Holten 'n figure he cain't run too fast after brother Blackwell here put a slug in his nether parts." Barlow turned his face into the wind. "He can hide in the darkness a Satan, but not from the flames o' the Lord's vengeance." Barlow lit his torch and trotted to the edge of the grass.

Eli looked up from the cover of the gully and saw the northern horizon lit by wind-blown flames. His heart pounded wildly as he tried to feature how far away the creek lay.

Chapter Eight

Nathan Barlow had to be the most rotten person the scout had ever encountered, he thought, as he watched the flames rise into the sky. How far the prairie fire would burn, how many lives it would cost, how many people and animals would go hungry were all in the hands of God.

Nathan had done this horrible act simply to destroy one man, Eli Holten. Eli wondered if he should feel guilty. He didn't. Rather his rage matched the fury of the wildfire he watched. For this, Nathan Barlow would pay, he and all who rode with him. For the first time, Eli had no intention of taking his man alive.

Grimly, Holten turned his back on the flames and began to hobble for the creek at top speed. Wind drove the blaze rapidly across the tinder-dry grass. As the conflagration roared across the land, smoke billowed up, obliterating moon and stars.

Holten was illuminated by an eerie orange glow, and the hot air bit at his lungs like the holocaust around him. He knew no fear, only consuming hatred and a desperate cunning that compelled him along the gully, falling, scrambling up only to pitch forwared again. The pain in his dragging leg kept him in touch with reality through bolts of agony delivered to his pounding skull.

Sincere regret ached in Nathan Barlow's heart as he watched the fire. Like a charging line of cavalry with bright red lances stabbing heavenward, it consumed the waving flesh of the prairie. For a moment the leaping flames died down, caught in an eddy of wind, and Barlow choked on the acrid smoke. He felt better about himself as the fumes dried his throat. The bandit leader prided himself on his morality. He hacked and coughed loudly to show he also suffered. No one could say Nathan Barlow was callous or placed himself above others.

"Harlan," he choked out, "take Art and ride west until you're upstream of the fire. Look for Holten ta come up the creek."

"Right, Boss," Harlan answered and began running for the horses as he called for Hawkins to join him. Shortly the two raised dust as they spurred away.

"A couple more of you boys ride between here and the creek. Look for Holten ta try ta run through the fire," the leader added.

"Smart thinking, Mr. Barlow," Jase Welles commented to his leader as he tended Jed's wound.

"How's my brother?" Nathan asked. Jed's face lacked any color, though the slug had merely left a deep furrow in the younger Barlow's upper arm. If the scout could do that off balance, in the dark, what the devil could he manage under good conditions?

"He'll be all right, Mr. Barlow," the hired shooter assured. "You boys are too tough to die from something like this."

Nathan looked to the flames in the south.

"I hope Holten's not too tough. The Good Book says, 'Give thanks, for with a mighty hand and an outstretched arm, His mercy endures forever.'"

Eli Holten looked back over his shoulder. He saw nothing but fire and smoke to either side and behind. His gully had presented no obstacle to the conflagration that roared down upon him. Hot burning ash fell on Holten's back and hat while heat and fumes gagged him.

A low, water-worn escarpment of white granite rose from the floor of the gully. Eli's twisted right ankle refused his weight as he started over. He fell across it to plunge down the other side, headfirst into icy cold water. Holten pushed off the bottom in startled panic, his head surfaced before his hands cleared the mud. Hell, he realized with a start, his legs hadn't even gone under. At that instant the fire roared over him.

It had leapt the creek and now moved on. The blessed coolnes of water surrounded him. It flowed! He'd made the creek. Alternately crawling and swimming, Eli moved downstream, his thoughts approaching blasphemy on the subject of how a man was always too damn hot or too damn cold. Then he remembered to that the great *Pta*, high spirit of the buffalo, for destroying the trees that would have made the fire unbearable along the creek bank.

As it was, the blaze had effortlessly stepped across the water and for a moment enveloped Eli in a great smoky cathedral of flame. Bush and heavier fuels still crackled along the smouldering banks, fouling the air to within inches of the water. Nathan Barlow had nearly ignited his funeral pyre, the scout conceded.

Eli's twisted ankle had long since been forgotten. He belatedly realized it was numb with cold. Shit, if the bone was broken he'd have a record-smashing case of rheumatism, another good reason to lynch Barlow. That was a hanging Eli did not intend to miss.

The banks cooled somewhat, and the flares of brush and buffalo chips burned far enough apart that Holten eased up the bank for an orientation sight on Stone Hollow. Fortunately the moon had found a chink in the now nearly uniform cloud cover. The pile of boulders looked grim and threatening through the haze. Wisps of smoke drifted across a landscape, punctuated by hotspots that heightened the eerie effect. Eli figured he had another mile to go. It would, thank God, take him well past where the fire burned languidly to the west, at the mercy of the wind, alternately flaring or blowing out the breadth of its long perimeter.

Hawkins and Bowes had been forced to move twice by the westward encroachment of the flames. They now sat, choking and gagging from the smoke the north wind picked up along the fire's westernmost line and drove into their faces. They endured this because firelight on the perimeter lit the water of the creek and would, should he come along, offer the best shot at the scout.

"Reckon anyone could'a got through that?" Bowes asked.

"Naw, I don't think so," replied Art Hawkins. "But then I got Nathan Barlow ta do muh thinkin' fer me. Ain't natcheral how often that man's right."

"If'n he comes up that crick," Harlan mused, "he ain't got a prayer."

Eli slipped a bit closer to the two men, pushing through the grass he'd sunk into. Nearby, a tired-looking oak hung precariously to the rise he spied from. The scout smiled to himself. He would wait a bit longer, then head for his horses. Holten thought about taking the two guards out, then dismissed the idea. He didn't want to let Barlow know he'd escaped. With any luck the gang would stay looking for him in the morning, and that would give the scout a good headstart toward Eagle Butte.

Suddenly Eli froze. He waited for a cold second, then lowered his face against the musty smelling grass.

Horses charged by the scout close enough to touch them, as three more gang members rode into the sentry post.

"You boys ready for a break?" the first man, Tony Cooper, shouted.

"Hell, yes," Bowes cursed back. "Anythin' happenin' ta camp?"

"You bet," the second rider, who liked to be called Slim, answered. "We found three beautiful Indian ponies and a real nice saddle and Winchester over yonder in a buffalo wallow."

"Holten's?" Harlan asked.

"Now who the hell else?" the third rider, a man known only as Tunney, answered tersely.

"He was runin' that lilly-livered Blackwell to ground," Harlan remarked with admiration. "I tell ya, that Holten is good."

"*Was* good if'n ya ask me," Tunney countered, looking out to the wild flames through the deadly smoke. "No man could'a survived that but the devil hisself."

"Well, then, you better watch yourselves," Cooper said with a laugh, " 'cause with all that fire, old Holten might feel right at home." His face became grimly serious. "Barlow was mightly impressed with Holten, how he got

102

past us and took out old Luke. The boss says ta keep yer eyes peeled on yerself and each other, as well as the crick. I think that's purty damn good advice. We're gonna keep runnin' riders out here 'til mornin' ever' hour're or so, checkin' the fire line to see if'n Holten snuck out here anywheres, and to make sure you boys're still alive." Cooper turned to the two relief sentries. "You'll git spelled in a little while. We got plenty a people fer guard duty, an' ever'one's gonna take their turn." Cooper looked sheepish. "Uh, by the way, boys, the boss says I gotta take yore hosses back with me. Hell, might save yore lives, that Holten fellow *is* mighty good."

Eli hardly heard the protests. His best chance for a horse had dissolved. He lay in the grass, searching for the "heart of the bear." The Indians believed the bear had a cool head and clear thoughts under the worst of times, and for the scout, times had certainly become bad.

Holten studied on his situation, and it seemed to get grimmer with every passing thought.

All alone, hurt, horseless, with his only weapons a six shooter and a knife, Eli's mind raced to find an escape and a means to get him back to Eagle Butte. Every way he figured, it looked impossible. He couldn't hope to walk away. Hell, he couldn't even stand without pain. He thought about sneaking down and stealing his horses back. The leg again got in the way, and besides, with the meticulous care Barlow took on the watch of the perimeter, the scout expected the same caution to be applied to the camp. Holten gave up some grudging respect to the bandit. He seemed to excel at the meticulous. With the number of men he had with him, Barlow could afford that. If Holten could only get them to spread out, he figured, he might stand a chance to take a horse away from some of these coyotes. Hah, how? Shoot the roving patrol out of the saddle? The fool horse would run off, leaving him in a barrel of hot water.

As if on cue, Cooper pressed on.

"Tomorrow bright an' early, we're gonna split up an' find Holten's body," the hired killer stated. "There's some things that Barlow wants to do to him, dead or alive."

Now Eli saw a desperate plan forming. It still had suicidal aspects with it, and it might take a miracle to work, but in his present condition, he'd gotten to praying some time back.

Holten was covered from head to foot with inky black soot. It suited his mood. He waited until Cooper rode off, using the clatter of the horse to cover any slight sound he might make, and took his own exit, moving further upstream. Considering the state of affairs the scout might as well get what rest he could. Tomorrow promised to be a lively day . . . or a fatal one.

Other eyes had seen the fire, eyes that glowed with righteous wrath.

Young War Pony stood close to his older brother, Lame Hawk. They were on a rise some two miles from Stone Hollow.

"There is no end to it," War Pony choked through his anger.

The smell of smoke had awakened the small Cheyenne hunting party of four untried braves. Three of them should have been warriors but adherence to treaties had deprived them of their birthright. The group stared silently, contempt and loathing swelling their heart, overburdened with wrongs, both real and fancied.

"Look how it burns," Hungry Wolf, exclaimed in awe, pointing to the far horizon where flames flickered for endless miles, smaller and less ominous in appearance because of distance and the curvature of the Earth.

"There is where it started," Lone Pine proclaimed.

Lame Hawk, leading his first hunting party, took note of the two converging lines that proclaimed the fire's origin.

"It was set. See how broad the front of its beginning is?"

"No one, not even the white man, could be that stupid," War Pony hedged.

"White men are not stupid, they are vicious. Now is the time of making meat for winter. They would starve us," growled Hungry Wolf.

"Then they are stupid," Lame Hawk reflected aloud. "The fire will hurt them worse than us. We can move to another hunting ground, as will the buffalo."

"Reasons no longer matter, it is done," put in Lone Pine. "They must be punished."

The hunters waited for their leader to speak. For them, this had been an adventure. They had formed their party in secret, elected the leader and stolen out of camp. At this moment they regreted the absence of older and wiser heads. "We shall ride down there at dawn," Lame Hawk finally announced. "We will learn what happened."

"Should we send War Pony for help?" asked Lone Pine.

Lame Hawk shot him an arrogant look. Cheyenne were raised to be self-sufficient.

"We will handle this, the honor shall be ours." And the *coups*, he prayed silently, anticipating new status as a warrior.

His Honor, Louis B. Thornton, straightened a string tie under his third chin, carefully arranged his "hanging expression," removed his pearl-gray Stetson, and marched into the sickroom of Marshal Peters.

Despite this preparation, his bulbous red nose wrinkled, and chubby, blue and red-veined jowls shivered at the sight of the dying lawman.

Peters lay in his bed. The windows had been tightly closed against the frigid fall wind, the smell of death clung to the room like moisture.

The jurist stepped to Peters' bedside, forgetting his carefully rehearsed monologue.

"Damn, Orsen," the Judge cursed, "you look awful."

"That's 'cause I am," the marshal whispered, his bloodless lips hardly moving.

Amy fought back tears as Doctor Andrews stepped back from her father's bed, his face grave.

"Is — is there anything I can do for you, sir?" the Judge asked. "I hate to leave. As you know, I was supposed to be at Lantry . . ."

"Stay," Peters begged. "When Holten gets back, you appoint him temporary marshal, so's he can hang that Blackwell bastard."

"I've tarried too long, Marshall," Thornton begged off. He forced a smile to his face. "Besides you'll be hanging that boy yourself. I shan't deprive you of that pleasure."

"Please," Peters pressed with the fading breath in his

lungs. "Then let the townsfolk hang him before Barlow gets here."

"Barlow is not coming here, my good man," the Judge replied with massive dignity that suddenly crumpled. "For the love of God, man. Would you ask me to sacrifice everything we've lived for, fought for?"

"He's guilty, guilty as sin," Peters wheezed. "Make him pay! It's our duty to make him pay!"

"Not outside the law," Thornton replied bluntly. He put his hat on the thrust forward his considerable front. "We fight for greater things, we must not tarnish the shining sword."

"If it's the last thing . . ." Peters paused and the stench of putrid flesh rose to his nostrils. "*It is going to be* the last thing I ever do, and so help me, I want to see Blackwell hang."

"Oh, Daddy!" Amy turned away and stifled a sob. Where, oh where, was Eli Holten?

Chapter Nine

The morning dawned dull red. Far to the south the horizon was blanketed in smoke extending deep to both east and west. Barlow rose after sleeping the sleep of the Just. He studied the burned creek banks with field glasses.

During the night the two-man watch on the stream had been relieved every two hours, keeping the sentries alert and wary. They had seen nothing.

"What we gonna do now, Nathan?" Jed asked, a slight fever breaking cold sweat on his brow.

"The Good Book says a man should be patient and thorough in all things," the elder Barlow replied. "Ah figure we better find that body. Ah don't want that scout behind us when we run against Peters."

"Nothin' could'a survived that fire," Jed scoffed. "He burnt up like a buffalo chip."

"Ah just want to see the body and cut the balls from it, that's all." Barlow snarled. "Ah said Ah'd do that and Nathan Barlow is a man of the Word." He chuckled suddenly, "Don' reckon his scrotum'll be worth a tinker's dam fer holdin' tobacco now though."

The rest of the men, roused by the conversation, crawled out and began rolling their blankets. Jake Day who doubled as camp cook for extra pay, had the coffee ready and was slicing bacon. While the men sipped experimentally from their tin cups, Nathan laid out his plans for the day.

"We start by combin' down the crick. Ah reckon thet's where we'll find Holten. If'n we don't, we'll spread out along the bank and work back to here. Blackwell, you're horse guard an' lookout. Should we flush him 'twixt here 'n the crick, you take him with that big Remington."

"He should be dead, right?" Jase Welles queried.

"Should be, don't get stupid and count on it," Barlow admonished.

"Nate!" Harry Lemley called down from lookout. "Injuns!"

The camp erupted quietly as the shootists scrambled for rifles and scattered into the rocks.

"Where?" Nate hissed. "How many."

"Only four," came the reply. "Due west."

"Hay, Welles, keep our hosses out a sight."

John and Jace slipped through the rocks to the east.

"Looks like young braves to me," Nathan mumbled to Jed a moment later. "Cheyenne and they's painted fer war, jest full a piss 'n vinegar. They'll be shootin' fer sure. Shit! They've tooken our creek guard."

Jed didn't need the commentary. He could plainly see the confrontation. The white gunmen, afoot, faced four armed and mounted Indians. They gestured frantically and kept their hands well away from weapons as all four bows of the young Indians had arrows nocked. The two terrified whites pointed several times to the rocks, while the braves continued to gesticulate.

As one, the bows were suddenly drawn.

The gunmen dropped their rifles and unbuckled belts, stepping reluctantly back from their weapons. A long delayed whoop reached the rocks. By the time it sounded the Cheyenne had scooped up the weapons and set about flailing the running hardcases with their bows, counting coup.

"All you men get well hid," Nathan growled across the rocks. "When I take off muh hat'n yell, open fire."

At first the Cheyenne didn't want to go to the rocks. They had two white men right here. Hungry Wolf was of the opinion they should scalp them to atone for the fire, even though without horses their fine weapons would make great trophies. Lame Hawk held them back and tried to question the prisoners. They seemed greatly frightened, hardly worth killing. Also they appeared to be trying to say the person who started the fire was in the boulders. Lame Hawk had no way of knowing, though he was determined not to leave armed whites behind him. Perhaps they would need these weapons. He gestured in sign language until sure of being understood, then realized the strangers were stalling.

They comprehended the drawn bows well enough. When the braves charged, these despicable ones threw away their pride and broke into an awkward run. Lame Hawk and Hungry Wolf scooped up rifles, crowding together so that the other two had to circle back to get the revolvers.

Lame Hawk was the first to count *coup*. He'd nearly struck the second man before the bow of Hungry Wolf slapped his first *coup*. When the ritual was over for him, Lame Hawk lined out toward the boulders at an easy lope, knowing the others would follow. Striking an unarmed enemy didn't count for much. Perhaps the elders would allow them to become warriors though, taking into consideration the limited opportunity that came with changing times. At least he, Lame Hawk, would make the grade with his first strike.

War Pony cantered up on his left and Hungry Wolf reined in next in line. Lone Pine fell in to the right, the positions predetermined to protect Lame Hawk's younger brother. War Pony did not know the real reason he was placed between the two strongest braves. He was simply content to ride beside his worshipped brother. Lame Hawk could see in his imagination what a fine spectacle they made. His first war party, gloriously painted, wearing their finest; and the ponies still pranced with the freshness of the morning. Shame about the soot dust; if the threatening clouds had released even a sprinkle their appearance would surely awe the whites.

Barlow stepped from the boulders and stood there, Tony concealed to the right and behind, where he could keep his eye on his boss.

"What's the plan, Mr. Barlow?"

"If we get caught anywhere near this fire by white or red man, we'll be hunted down by every damn sinner in the Dakotas," Nathan answered. "None o' those heathen better leave here alive."

Nathan felt the Remington .44 press against his spine. He'd left his belt and holster behind. The outlaw stood hipshot and absently watched the Cheyenne approach, careful to look neither right nor left and give the inexperienced bucks any reason for suspicion. He spread on a horse-toothed, crooked grin.

War Pony and Lone Pine carried the pistol belts slung over their left shoulders, revolver butts forward. Both carried bows in hand, arrows nocked. Lame Hawk, like

Hungry Wolf, slanted the unfamiliar Winchesters across his pony's shoulders. All had left their high wooden saddles in camp.

The transition from hunt leader to war leader and his recent *coup* made Lame Hawk haughty and brave beyond his talents, yet he studied the rocks carefully, taking his responsibility seriously. Lame Hawk could see another man standing behind the one with beaver teeth who waited for them. This other white looked wounded, perhaps there had been a fight.

"That one does not look badly hurt, War Pony. If there is trouble he is yours."

Nathan reached for his hat with his left hand as the right dipped behind him.

"Now!"

Ten professional shooters reared from hiding with tuned weapons poised.

War Pony had his man. He could tell even as his left arm drew the bow in swift, practiced motion. Suddenly something struck his weapon a terrific blow. The upper limb of the bow separated and slammed the young warrior between the eyes. Instantly he grabbed for his pony's mane to save his seat, the shattered weapon still in his tingling right fist.

Lame Hawk didn't see his brother's troubles, as the obvious leader, the accomplished Indian fighters in the gang, concentrated on him. Four bullets struck him from many divergent angles.

Cooper took him from below, through the sternum, and blew out a section of spine. A large chunk of his throat dissolved in a red mist when Lemley's bullet passed down through it from his open, screaming mouth, and Ham Jenkins placed one that traveled from bellybutton to anus, breaking his horse's spine before stopping between its kidneys. The last two hundred five grain slug blasted through the back of Lame Hawk's neck, nearly severing the head before he could fall. A turkey-necked backshooter named Slim Cranston could claim credit for that one.

Chub Kennedy put the first hole in Hungry Wol. It slammed into his shoulder with enough force to knock him from the path of other slugs that riddled his pony. The Cheyenne warrior began his death song, even as he jacked another round into the Winchester to replace the unaimed bullet he'd reflexively fired.

Lone Pine, too, had drawn his bow, the release spoiled by a .44 slug from the Whitneyville Kennedy carbine in the hands of Shank O'Niel. The freakish hit burned between the second and third fingers of his left hand, striking through the knuckle bones to split the palm, then shattered half a dozen intricate wrist bones, exiting the arm at that point and lodging in the hinge of his jaw. Lone Pine felt nothing but shock and disappointment in the altered trajectory of his arrow. Big Jack Glenn's bullet eliminated his worry when it entered above Lone Pine's ear and finished removing his jaw.

In total panic the half-trained pony of Lone Pine milled across the front of the war party, shielding the two remaining warriors from Nate and Jed Barlow, who had so far been unable to find a target that would hold still. Even as the killers were levering fresh rounds into their repeaters, War Pony's mount spun, throwing him off to the side away from the ambush, where he clung like a burr as his terrified animal carried him out of the fight.

Unkowing, War Pony had nearly run down Hungry Wolf who was trying to charge the Barlows, breaking the impetus of his effort. Both Nathan and Jed emptied their guns into Hungry Wolf the moment they had a clear shot, then watched in fascinated horror as he staggered in a circle, only to again bring his rifle to bear.

Hungry Wolf's final shot triggered a volley from seven more rifles, the bullets from which literally blew him apart. His own lead passed harmlessly between the brothers. He had provided an awesome distraction. War Pony gained over two hundred feet, thanks to the valiant death of Hungry Wolf.

"Get that heathen!" roared a shaken Nathan. He, Jed, and Cooper did not have a clear field of fire.

Once again the rifles high up in the rocks began to blast, each man firing as he judged angle and lead to be correct.

War Pony hadn't any idea what had happened. All he knew for sure was that an awful lot of whites in the rocks had opened fire unexpectedly and he was in deep trouble. If he could break free, get to his father, they would return and show those *slukas* what a real Cheyenne war party looked like.

The first bullet connected. There had been others which had closely missed, accurate enough to tell War Pony he would not make it as they kicked up hunks of prairie sod around him. The next took his valiant little pony in the hip with a meaty smack that sent shock waves through horse and rider. Two more rounds followed in rapid succession. Still the animal plowed ahead. They had covered nearly a hundred yards when another slug brought a death scream from the little stud and they dropped in a heap.

War Pony knew he had reached extreme range for the outlaws' .44-40s. One man had a bigger rifle as could be told from its harsher boom and the larger bullet strikes he had seen; fortunately that person was not a very good shot. The young warrior began to run.

Bart Blackwell took careful aim. The big Remington bellowed and slammed back hard on the scrawny outlaw's shoulder. Another miss. Damn that little redskin, why wouldn't he run in a straight line? Bart fired five more shots, flinching from the brutal recoil but giving up only when the other bandits began to jeer at him.

"Get them damned hosses around heah!" bellowed Nate. "All of yuh come down heah. We gotta get that damned savage before he brings the whole territory down on our heads. Blackwell, you incompetent shit! Yore the guard for the spare hosses, fuck that up, I'll skin yuh." Nathan turned and began a clumsy lope around the boulders. "C'mon, let's get mounted."

Hay and Welles nearly ran Barlow down with the horses they'd taken the precaution of saddling. The steady, slow booming of Blackwell's .45-70 had told them at least one Indian escaped. It required no genius to deduce the animals were needed in a hurry.

"John! You boys get after that red bastard. We'll be right behind yuh, " the elder Barlow instructed. "Nathan!" Jed called as he hopped in circles with one foot in the stirrup, trying to get in position to swing up on his skittish gelding. "What about Holten?"

"When those two sentries get up here they can pick up their guns and look fer Holten," Nathan roared into the dust and confusion. "When we get that Injun we'll ride

115

direct fer Eagle Butte. Deliver Holten's balls to me there."

Jed had finally gained his seat. White-faced and cursing all horseflesh, he spoke another thought to his brother.

"What if them Injuns was part of a big huntin' party? They could'a heard the shootin'."

"It's the Lord's will we make Eagle Butte pay," Nate answered loudly as he spurred next to his brother. Then in a lower register, "They didn't have no older bucks with 'em. They snuck off from a village somewheres."

Nate caused his horse to rear.

"Yahhhoooooo! This bunch a ring-tailed hardcases could chop up the whole Sioux Nation. Bring 'em on."

The Barlow Gang charged off on Nathan's sacred mission.

Chapter Ten

The bark of rifles and the screams of men and horses woke Eli from his fitful sleep. He jumped and felt needles of pain jab up through his leg. Eli scrambled to the top of the creek bank and chose a low bush to poke his head up under. The scout looked across the perimeter of the stream to the rock pile, he could see nothing moving. The fight must be on the other side or in the center, at Barlow's camp.

Thoughts of Barlow, coupled with the distant shots, made him uneasy. Slowly, the firing died out, ending with the slow, steady boom of what Eli took to be Blackwell's big Remington, the sound rolling ominously across the expanse of ground separating him from the scene of action. The scout made a quick inventory of his condition.

The right leg moccasin still strained with the swollen foot. All the same, Eli noted groggily, it hadn't gotten worse and he felt at least rested. His eyes stung and grated with accumulated ash, and his throat felt as though someone had shoved a rasp down it. His hands were worn raw. He longed for a long, cool drink and his stomach protested its emptiness. All in all, he considered himself not too badly off. Then he took stock of the situation he had gotten into.

Why had he conceived a plan so desperate and full of

holes? In the cold light of early morning he wasn't quite sure of what had convinced him that it would work. Or that it would work at all. On the previous evening, he had made note of the black soot that covered him from head to toe. That had fostered the idea. The risk he discounted. His life had been continually at hazard since the age of fifteen. From a distance, he knew, he would look like he'd been burned to death, blending in with the ruined prairie. It should, he thought then, give him the opportunity to let anyone Barlow sent to check on him get close enough for a silent kill. The unexplained gunfire of earlier nagged at him. Had the gang members quarreled and turned on each other?

Eli hobbled up the embankment and peered over in the direction of the boulders. Still nothing moved. He could only guess.

Not being an inveterate gambling man, Holten chafed at his lack of knowledge and the foolhardiness of his plan in the face of that weakness. He studied his Bowie knife. It had saved his life last night. He'd look to it today. Right now he had a lot of ground to cover. Holten slid down the bank and noted with satisfaction that the waters of the creek had cleared. He took his long, cold drink, then began to wade downstream, back through the burn.

Tunney scratched at his three-day-old stubble, then squinted over at Bill. "What do you figure's so important about this here Holten feller?" he asked his companion as they walked their horses westward. "After killin' them Injun kids, I say we're takin' a mighty big risk for the sake of capturin' one man."

"From what I heard," Bill answered, "Holten caught the Barlow boys dead to rights without firin' a single shot. Grabbed the whole gang. Nathan took that sorta personal."

Tunney thought on that for a moment or two, frowned, and shook his head. "No man, short a Satan hisself, could catch Nathan Barlow cold. An' like I said, I don't hanker to lose my scalp while lookin' fer a feller who's more'n likely nothin' but a crispy critter by now."

"We'd best be careful, then," Bill countered. "He worked awful slick on Louie last night. So if he's alive out there, we got him *and* the Injuns to worry about."

Eli checked his Remington one more time. The scout worried about the corrosion that might be setting in to his precious shooting iron. He checked the sharp, wet, blade of his Bowie and felt reassured. He wiped the knife on his pants' leg. It did little good, though it did make him feel more prepared. Whatever had happened on the circle of rocks had to affect him, he reasoned. Though that sure didn't give him reason to abandon caution.

In spite of his condition, Holten was a little surprised when he came upon the granite lip at the mouth of his gully. The events of the previous night had the time distortion quality of a nightmare.

Carefully he raised his hatless head above the lip of the draw. His cold, blue-gray eyes scanned the blackened land around him. Thin wisps of smoke rose here and there. In the distance he saw indistinct movement. Slowly the distant images resolved into two men on horseback. Hunters. Tall against the gray sky, looking for him.

The scout gazed all around and couldn't spot the

other men he'd seen last night. One of the big problems with his strategy was that there were so many of them. Now only two appeared and that seemed a more manageable number. Holten slid down to the bottom of the draw. A new plan cooked slowly and evenly in his mind.

The two rifle-toting gunmen rode to the edge of the fire, where the sentries had been waiting before the arrival of the Cheyenne boys. There they reined in. Bill squinted toward the sun, then across the blackened earth.

"Where you figger we're gonna find 'im?" he asked.

Tunney didn't answer for a while, eyes on the unbroken smear of black. Then he smiled and nodded toward the burned prairie. "Where he got fried, that's where we'll find him." He touched heels to his horse's flanks and started down toward the creek.

Bill and Tunney found nothing there and swung to the southeast for nearly a mile, locating burned quail, rabbits, and prairie chickens, but no Eli Holten. With each passing second they expected to see a swarm of enraged Cheyenne warriors come up over the rise, bent on vengeance and armed to their eyeballs.

"This is stupid," Tunney growled. "We're lookin' fer some fried army meat that ain't gonna do us no harm whether we find him er not."

"Barlow wants him," Bill responded.

"Barlow won't know if we just leave now an' say we found Holten there in the creek, right where Barlow said he'd be." Tunney pointed across the length of the burned ground.

"Barlow wants us to bring his balls back." Bill answered.

"Look at all that, would ya?" Tunney countered, ignoring Bill's response. "We're searchin' fer someone all burned up. Everythin' done burnt up. Where the hell do we start?"

"If he ain't here in the creek," Bill replied as he studied the terrain in back of him, "then he di'n't make it down here, else he woulda stayed."

Tunney grimaced at Bill's simplistic logic, then grudgingly nodded. "Still a lotta ground to cover," he finally answered. "We better split up, or I swear we'll be here 'til spring."

Elil wiped more of the fluffy, sticky ash over his face to give it a charred appearance. He knew they'd look for him in the draw after examining the obvious places. Now Holten realized the prairie grass had been hiding a regular gully that angled east to west until it wandered out of sight. Four feet deep and it ran forever. Such hazards were common enough on the plains; it had only been his misfortune to encounter one at the wrong time.

Holten struggled again to the top of the draw, a painful crawl that ached his swollen leg and sent blinding pain up into his groin when he tried to put weight on it. No doubt about it, Eli thought. He'd have to stay and fight . . . he couldn't run.

The scout could see far down the creek. Two figures rode back to the west, their search of that area completed. Eli licked his lips. Every bone in his body ached. He'd forgotten all about his wounded butt. Now it flared up again, hurting like a toothache. While he watched, the gunslingers split up.

Tunney held to the north side of the creek while Bill aimed for the rocks. They twisted their heads from side to side, in search of a lump large enough to be a man. Slowly Bill neared Eli's position.

Eli slid back down to his spot, studied the aspects of his desperate plan, then lay down and played fried. He slipped his knife out of its sheath and held it under his body.

Bill angled toward the gully. He headed west along its bank, looking for a place to cross. All the time he inspected the bottom of the draw, made note of more animal corpses, and glanced from time to time at his distant partner.

Another carcass lay ahead. Larger than the others. Ash-covered, it lay sprawled against the far side of the gulch, lifelessly still. Bill squinted, smiled and dismounted. He drew his Winchester from its boot. He took two steps closer to verify his discovery, then looked up from the creek.

"Hey, Tunney," Bill shouted. "I think I found our boy."

Tunney reined his horse around and ambled toward where Bill stood.

The dismounted gunman ran to where he overlooked the body and cackled to himself as he leaned over to get a better view of the ash-covered human form.

"Hey, Holten!" he mocked the burned body. "That you?"

As Bill rolled the corpse over, a knife appeared in Holten's hand and slithered through the air with a whispering whir. "Yes, it is," the scout answered agreeably.

Bill's jaw sagged, but no sound came from his mouth. He dropped his repeater and it clattered onto the sandy bottom of the draw. The gunman's lips worked open and shut like a fish, as his hands reached for the Bowie knife that was buried to its hilt in his sternum. He staggered, trying not to fall backwards. Instead he fell headfirst into the gulch and rolled against Eli.

The scout grabbed up the Winchester at his feet, pulled his Bowie free of Bill's chest, and wiped it on the dead man's pants' leg. Eli sheathed the knife, then crawled over the twitching gunman and up the side of the draw.

Tunney brought his horse to a halt. Bill had suddenly disappeared into the gully and it hadn't looked right. He reconnoitered the vacant horizon. Bill's mount stood patiently waiting for its master to return. Tunney urged his own forward and he advanced cautiously to where Bill had gone into the crack in the earth.

A head popped up along the ridge and Tunney felt relief. Old Bill must be playing games, the gunman thought. He let his breath sigh out . . . and missed the first crack of the Winchester.

Fiery lead caught his right shoulder, blowing a fat, nasty tear in the hired gunman. Tunney's horse whinnied and bucked at the noise. A cool head and a stout, mean heart kept the man from panicking. He grasped the situation even as he fought to stay in the saddle. He gained control, turned his mount west and slammed his heels into the animal's sides.

Eli wetted his lips and sighted the wounded rider as he turned away. Holten compensated for the moving target, then squeezed the trigger. The repeater barked and another .44-40 slug took to the air, flying fast and true.

This time the hot lead caught Tunney in the side. It slammed in low enough to miss his lungs, though it ripped through his large intestine and liver before popping out through a rib.

The expended energy of the bullet also blew the gunman off his horse. He hit the ground with a burbling scream, the belly wound strangling him with pain.

Eli ignored the noise. He crawled over the ledge to hop and hobble to Bill's horse.

The animal's eyes rolled, wild and terrified. The gunplay had spooked the riderless animal and now a black stranger stumbled toward the trembling beast.

Eli stopped and took stock of himself. Any horse worth its oats would have run for cover the moment it spied something that looked like him coming at it. If Bill's mount broke and ran, though, Holten thought, he'd surely die trying to get it back.

"Whoa, horse," Eli cooed. He smiled through the ash on his face, stopped as the critter backed away. All the while, he kept talking.

"I'm harmless, horse. I wanna make friends," Eli offered. He leaned on the barrel of his acquired Winchester.

"Wuh, huh, huh, huh, huh, easy partner, huh, huh, huh."

Eli continued to sooth the tall gray with Indian 'horse talk' as he inched forward, holding his hand out as though it held some treat.

The animal's curiosity was piqued. His nostrils fluttered at the distant hand. Then he moved cautiously closer, suspiciously eyeing Eli, while he flapped his lips in anticipation.

Holten snatched the bit and the gray reared, dragging him from his precarious balance. Eli held fast as his life did depend on it.

"Whoa, whoa girl, steady, steady now." The mare settled down and the scout regained his feet. Still tightly gripping the bit, he breathed into her nostrils. Holten sighed with relief. He stuck the Winchester in his boot, then used his good leg to swing himself into the saddle. The now familiar agony of needles racing up his calf into his grion left the scout reaching for breath.

He waited until the pain subsided, then urged the horse toward the screaming Tunney. Eli leaned over and studied the dying man on the ground.

Tunney looked up through eyes glazed with pain. His rifle still hung on his horse. He reached for his revolver, which stuck out of his belt, but the wounded right shoulder robbed him of the strength to pull it out. The gunhawk tried to roll over to get his other hand to the weapon. All that did was force some of his savaged entrails out through the gaping hole in his side. His face twisted into whole new meanings of agony.

Holten thought about dismounting and retrieving the clean revolver. He'd left the other bandit's handgun with its owner. The idea of going through all that pain ruled out the possibility of the action. Eli considered finishing this gunman off. He dismissed that, too. Why waste a bullet? Besides, any more shooting might attract unwanted attention.

"Kill me," Tunney cried. "The pain's so bad."

"I thought about that," Eli answered blandly. "But I really can't afford the ammo. Could be, too, that all the shootin' might get Barlow and the rest of the gang over here. I'd like to avoid that."

"They took off," Tunney volunteered. "They left me'n Bill to find ya."

"And so you did," Eli replied. "Where is Nathan headed?"

"To Eagle Butte. He wants to even things with the marshal."

"What else does he intend to do?"

"Figgers to burn the town down around those yokels' heads." Tunney blanched and a trickle of blood ran from his mouth. "Oh, God, this hurts."

"A new man join up with you lately?"

"Y-yeah. Yesterday. Said you was chasin' him."

"I am." Satisfied that he had learned all he could, Eli gently heeled the horse with his good leg and headed for the creek. "Thanks for the information."

"Kill me!" Tunney shrieked. "For the love of God!"

Eli didn't look back. At the babbling water, he finally did dismount and painfully stripped to clean himself and his clothes. About the time he finally got his hair washed, Tunney's distant screaming stopped.

War Pony's lungs burned like the prairie fire that put the young brave where he found himself. He ducked and swerved through the brambles that tore at his flesh. His people's village lay to the north and he headed that way.

For most of the morning he had evaded the thirteen men that methodically searched for him. More than a few times he had been sure he had lost his pursuers. The Indian backtracked twice through small creeks and camoflaged himself in mud to look like a wolf. Many times the whitemen fired at him in the distance, then stepped over his hiding place as they drew closer to search for him. War Pony took time in his desperate maneuvers to thank *Ah-badt-dadt-deah*, his God, for the skills his father and uncles had taught him so carefully.

By sheer numbers, and the skillful direction of their

leader, the whitemen closed the gap the Cheyenne had worked so hard to gain. By midday the young warrior could hear the voices of his pursuers and his strength seemed to wane in the never-easing chase. The plains offered few real places to hide, none of them permanent.

Then the youthful warrior-to-be realized he not only fled to his people, but also drew the killers closer to them. With three less braves, that only left seven other warriors in the camp. Considering the large number of whitemen with their fine weapons, the Cheyenne could not hope to stand against them.

War Pony suddenly remembered his dream-walking, where he reached for the bow string in the grandfather's hand. When he pulled away, he found a *coup* stick as well as the gut cord in his hand. The medicine man said he would count many *coups* in battle. Now, though, the young warrior thought perhaps this foretold his death.

He did not fear the whitemen. He only regretted none of his people would be there to see his glory as he prepared to die under a lone elm that clung tenaciously to a slight rise.

Nathan Barlor himself spotted the young Cheyenne this time, resting under the tree.

"There he is, boys!" Barlow shouted as he pointed with the muzzle of his rifle.

War Pony rose from under the tree, put his newly acquired revolver aside and tightly grasped the lower limb of his shattered bow. It would have to serve as a *coup* stick. He waved it at high speed in front of him. It whistled like a whip. War Pony frowned at not having a proper *coup* stick like in his dreams. Yet, he decided, this might be better. Making good medicine out of bad. Would anyone, he wondered, ever carry the story of his stand back to his people?

The gang members whooped gleefully as they charged the rise, spreading out until they encompassed three sides. Arrogantly the Cheyenne youth waited, studying the approaching whitemen and deciding his tactics.

Cooper made it up the hill first. He held his Colt revolver in his right hand and reined in on his horse with his left. None of the rustlers fired. The boy had put his gun down and seemed to ignore approaching death with only mild interest, for what reason only another savage could guess. The leader of the hired guns planned to be close enough to make the first shot end this chase.

With only a yard separating them, Cooper pointed his weapon at the unmoving target as his horse pranced to a stop. The bastard redman wasted the whole morning for the gang and Cooper took that personally.

"Die ya little shit!" Tony cursed at his victim.

Suddenly War Pony charged the shouting whiteman's horse, then began to weave and duck. The surprised gunman tried to correct his aim, holding his fire.

War Pony slipped with cougarlike speed under Cooper's mount, came up behind and brought the Osage orange bow down hard across the whiteman's back. Tony yelped, more from surprise than pain, though the solid wooden stave raised a considerable welt. He tried to turn and, in the same motion, fired.

The youngster stepped behind Cooper's horse and the slug only spooked the animal. It jumped and War Pony charged Nate Barlow's surging mount as Cooper wrestled with the crow-hopping horse.

Barlow brought his altered 1860 Remington .44 to bear on the running boy and fired.

The bullet caught Way Pony in the shoulder. It knocked his scapula out of joint.

War Pony staggered and knew, as more whitemen closed on him, that he would soon die. He called up every ounce of his strength and charged again at Barlow. Nate cocked his weapon, but not before the Cheyenne youngster slapped a stick across the rustler's chest.

Surprise registered on Barlow's face. He gritted his teeth and aimed again at the apparently mad young Indian who staggered at the neck of his horse.

War Pony started singing his Death Song and knew he died with great honor. Unarmed and on foot, he had counted *coup* on two armed, mounted whitemen. If only someone from his band could have seen him, he thought. Then his name would be spoken around every campfire, in every lodge, for many moons. Perhaps for winters.

Barlow's Remington put an end to the child-warrior's thoughts of glory. The outlaw leader fired again and hit War Pony square between the eyes, blowing the back of the boy's head off. He fell back onto the ground and started twitching.

"Crazy Injun," Cooper grunted out, rubbing his back where the bow had struck.

"Don't no one ever tell me these people ain't savages," Barlow answered. "They surely must be the '*axemen and swordsmen of Satan*' that the Good Book talks about. Now, boys, we ride for Eagle Butte."

Chapter Eleven

Eli easily rounded up the horse that had belonged to the now-silent gunhand and took the two animals to Stone Hollow. Ten yards outside the rocks he found three bodies, Cheyenne boys in their early to mid-teens.

"Goddamn Barlow and all his kind," the scout swore aloud. This sort of senseless, useless killing could get another uprising going. Conditions were bad enough for the Sioux and Cheyenne, his thoughts continued. It would take very little to draw the bow strings and set the scalping knives to being honed. With mounting anger he moved on, reading the signs left behind by the fleeing outlaws.

A dead horse lay further to the north, shot from a distance as it ran. He found no other body, though. From the indications, Holten could make a fairly good guess at what happened. Also why Barlow left only two men behind to search for him. Although Barlow had not hesitated to murder the boys, the wily rustler had sense enough not to seriously split his command in the event of retaliation by the Cheyenne. Eli saw small moccasin prints in the gray-brown soil and hoped the youngster escaped. He urged his mount to where he had left his three horses.

As experience told him, the ponies lent him by Big Wolf were long gone, along with his saddle and belongings. He checked the supplies that the dead hired guns no longer needed. Meager, Eli decided. He had the one shootist's Winchester, a well-kept machine that needed no repairs to make it acceptable. And his Remington, loaded and ready for close-in work. The killers carried plenty of ammunition. His survey revealed a major deficiency.

They lacked food. They hadn't planned to be on the prairie for long. He had been happy to oblige them, Eli mused, by sending them on to that place where they would never hunger. It left him somewhat cramped, for the food supply would not last to Eagle Butte, which meant he'd have to take time out to hunt. Thought of the town and the Barlow gang riding for it made the urgency of his situation press on his consciousness. He had to get there, and fast. And he could use any help he could get.

The good Reverend Zeke Smith, Eli thought. Quickly he studied the clear trail made by the large number of horses that carried the Barlow gang. First the tracks went west, then northwest, then due north. The Cheyenne boy ran on foot and Eli feared that not even the most experienced brave — which this youngster clearly was not — could escape such a body of men, especially under the canny, competent command of Nathan Barlow.

Still the trail led away from the northwest, the direction Smith and the pack mules would be coming from. If the gang missed the preacher, that would provide another gun, food, and reserve mounts. Perhaps that way he could beat Barlow to Eagle Butte. Eli swung into the saddle and pursued the trail, eyes alert for any sign of his missing supplies.

A slight bit more than half an hour later, something tickled at the scout's nostrils. Wood smoke. Tinged with the odors of cooking. His stomach rolled and grumbled.

He hadn't eaten since the previous day and, goaded by the scent of food being prepared close at hand, he felt weak with hunger. Holten put his heels to the unfamiliar horse and headed due south, in the direction of the mouth-watering aroma.

Cautiously the scout dismounted below a rise, then half limped, half crawled until he looked over the crest. Tendrils of white smoke escaped a rusty tin stovepipe.

A handsome homestead spread out from the bottom of the slope. Crops to the east and a sturdy corral and small barn to the west. A fence of native fieldstone separated the farmyard from a garden patch in front of the house. A few faded fall flowers struggled to exist in window boxes under the narrow openings set in the facing wall. A more inviting scene he could not imagine.

Eagle Butte, Eli reminded himself. Peters and Eagle Butte had to be warned.

His leg ached and he knew it needed better attention than he had been able to provide for himself. His head swam from hunger and lack of sleep. Blood loss weakened him further. He had been burned, bounced, shot at, and run ragged since he saw those damned rocks at Stone Hollow. He had to allow himself a decent meal before he continued his journey. He crawled, then hobbled back down to the two horses.

The scout mounted the gray he had made friends with and took the reins of the other. He crested the rise and ambled down to the yard. It sported a dozen chickens and a brace of ducks, all busy scratching at the ground and gabbling in their fowl languages. Two more red-beaked ducks frolicked in a neat and tidy water trough under the nozzle of an iron hand pump. As he neared, his eyes searched out any potential hiding places and sought any sign of habitation beyond the smoke rising thinly into the morning sky. He saw no one.

To his left a milk cow peered out at him from the sturdy, weather-grayed barn. Listening carefully, Eli heard sounds not quite right for a barnyard. Through the grunts of pigs and clucks of hens, the scout filtered out frantic sounds that made him think of women or older children panicking or in desperate straights.

Holten urged his horse silently while he removed the hammer retaining strap from his Remington, and loosened it in the holster. His instincts stretched out to feel for danger. Carefully he swung out of the stirrups and advanced on the ground.

Though his leg ached beyond description, he carefully hobbled around the barn to the open entrance, drawing his revolver. At the wide double doors, the sounds came more insistently, desperately. Significantly female sounds, although perhaps gagged or choking.

The interior of the barn had been laid out with the same care as the rest of the homestead. Rope and leather plow harness hung neatly from hooks to the side. Sturdily built stalls filled with clean hay supplied homes for a milk cow, a mule, an ox, and a horse. Eli hadn't seen such riches in a simple homestead in his life. He marveled at the bountiful plenty, until the muffled sounds became louder, more urgent, and brought the scout back to why he was there. Eli felt sure the noises came from humans, positively young ones . . . and female.

It crossed Eli's mind that someone might be in the hay with his girl. The mewings and whimpers could be caused by such an encounter. They could also, he reminded himself, come from a victim of the Barlow gang's special attentions. He listened attentively for another moment and heard no sounds that a man in the throes of passion would make. Curious, he determined to find the cause.

Cautiously, Eli edged along the side of the structure, his Remington cocked and leading the way. He slipped under the cow's munching jaw, eased himself to the next paddock. From there he could get his bearings.

The impassioned sounds came from an empty stall at the back of the barn. Eli moved silently to the second from the last cubicle and eased carefully into the opulant plank-sided stable alongside the horse, who seemed to take little interest in the goings-on next door. Holten peeked over the wooden wall and stopped breathing.

Two slender, cream-white forms struggled on the light yellow hay, their sausage roll curl-covered heads thrust deeply between each other's legs. Soft gurglings rose from among the pink petals of their matching young mounds. The pair's hair shone like the light golden hay they rolled in. Their firm, tight, naked buttocks tensed with each other's hungry ministrations at the opening of their sensual channels.

From what Eli could see, they appeared to be perfect copies of one delightful young female, turned end for end and linked by sinuous tongues. Mirror images of lean, white flesh, slick with moist passion sweat that undulated in unison with a building tempo that promised a sudden explosion into completion. Muffled moans and high, almost begging sounds emanated from their active lips. Four shapely legs flailed the air in ecstasy.

Eli slipped back down into the horse's quarters,

tipped back the brim of his hat and gave a moment's serious thought to what he had seen while his trousers tightened as his swelling member increased to match his damaged foot. Definately *not* the Barlow gang.

He reholstered his .44 and had a struggle of his own as he resisted drawing his other, fleshly gun that gained bore width and barrel length with each new, sensational moan.

"Oh! . . . Oh-oh, it's working, Sybil!" a young, muffled voice cried from beyond the divider.

"Y-yes . . . It's . . . won-wonderful, Samantha. I can feel what you're feeling," another dulcet voice gasped out. "A-an' what I'm feeling. . ."

"And what we both feel," the first girl squealed.

"Ah . . . aaah . . . AAAH! It's *fun* being twins!"

The town of Eagle Butte faced terror and brutalities at the hands of the Barlow gang. The marshal and the townsfolk had to be warned, Holten kept reminding himself. Resolutely, he steeled himself to the ordeal.

Less quietly now, Holten moved to the middle of the center aisle and, telling himself Eagle Butte came first, he walked away from the two beautiful girls so avidly dickering with each other.

"Stay right where you are, stranger," a cold female voice called out from behind him.

The scout tensed, then slowly turned. He looked down the double barrels of a fat Parker shotgun. The murderous weapon pointed from a door at the back of the barn. It did not waver as the woman behind it aimed for Eli's chest.

"Mama!" one of the girls cried out. Her duplicate looked out from between her sister's legs. "Mama!" she echoed.

135

The girls, in a panicked flurry, began to unwind and reach for a pair of matching blue dresses that hung neatly on hooks inside the stall.

"Samantha! Sybil!" the woman with the scatter gun spat curtly. "You don't move neither."

Both girls froze, their beautiful blue eyes full of surprised worry at the building wrath of their mother. Eli raised his hands.

"Get over here, stranger," Mama ordered her prisoner. She motioned toward her with the oversized weapon in her small hands. Her hair, Eli noted, matched the color of her daughters'. Her blue eyes shot disdain at Holten as he stepped forward. She cast a look at the girls that could tear the heart out of any child.

"Mama," one of the naked lovelies started. "We was only . . . playin'."

Mother's lip curled in anger and disgust for the speaker. The girl blanched and turned her eyes away. The older woman returned her cold stare to Eli. "You got a name, stranger?"

"Eli Holten, ma'am. Chief scout for the Twelfth Cavalry," Holten answered. "I didn't have anything to do with what was goin' on. Only just now dropped by to ask after a meal and some doctorin'." They were, on closer examination, extremely young. "I didn't. . ."

"Shut your mouth, Holten," the woman snapped. Exhaustion from taut emotion ached in her words. "My name's Susan Duddles. And these *fine* . . . creatures are my daughters, Sybil and Samantha."

Both girls, kneeling in the hay side by side, blushed as they tried to hide their nakedness with their hands, in mirror copies of each other. Sybil used her left hand to hide her breasts and the right her golden-furred mound.

The other used her right hand to cover her breasts, the opposite to hide the thatch of burly yellow-white hair between her legs. Otherwise they appeared alike, identical. From what Eli could see, there was no way of telling them apart.

"They're twins, iffin ya haven't guessed as yet," Susan continued. "They've always been close. *That's* natural for twins. This other ah . . . habit's fairly new, an' has become a problem only recently."

"Sounds to me like a family problem," Eli answered her evenly. "I was ridin' by and smelled your cookin' fire. I haven't eaten for days, it seems. I rode in lookin' for a meal," he repeated his earlier explanation.

Susan snickered through a crooked smile. "Oh, we'll feed ya," she remarked. "Later. Right now, you're gonna solve this little problem for me, Mister Holten. You happened by at a most opportune moment." She sounded old and tired, despite her own beautiful curves that tugged provocatively at the light green cotton work dress she wore. "Samantha, honey, go over there and take down his trousers."

A cream-white piece of warm, firm fluff scurried eagerly to Eli's side and gingerly tugged at the buckle of his cartridge belt. Her deep cerulean eyes looked lonely and terribly hungry as she gazed up at the scout. Once the heavy leather band came free, she started to back off.

"Stay right there, girl. Now, unlace them buckskins and let's see what our prize stud has betwixt his legs."

A fire of eagerness glowed in Samantha's eyes as she reached for the scout's leather thong-laced breeches. He took a quick step backward.

"Wait a minute. I . . . you . . . we can't be doing this. Eagle Butte."

137

"What about it?" Susan demanded.

"It's in danger. I have to get there quickly to warn the people."

"Injun uprising?"

"Uh, no. Outlaws."

"Well, then, you can take time out to help me teach these girls what they should have learned three, four years ago. Go on, Samantha."

The lovely young nude's small fingers dug at the ties and quickly freed the large front flap of Holten's trousers. He raised a hand in protest and the shotgun centered between his eyes.

"Mrs. Duddles, I'm in a genuine hurry. I'm in pain and I'm hungry. I really must tend to my needs and ride on."

Susan Duddles ignored his protest. "Now open 'em up, sweetheart."

Little Samantha looked hopefully up at Eli. Sybil straightened from her kneeling position in the stall. Her hands fell to her sides to expose small, satiny breasts that sat high on her youthful chest, their nipples reddened from her sister's recent stimulation, and, still erect, pointed now at Holten's face. Eli looked down at Samantha and saw the twin's form at a different angle. His partially extended lance stiffened another notch.

"Ma'am," Eli asked gently. "Just what in hell is it you have in mind?"

Susan Duddles sighed and swayed a bit. "I tried to tell my husband before he left for Midland that somethin' had to be done. They have to get broken in." She sagged with the weight of her maternal burden. "I tried to talk him into doin' it, but he'd have none of that. That don't solve nothin'. Fact is they've been growing more, uh,

138

itchy for each other over the past five years." Mother Duddles gained her strength back, determination fired in her blue eyes.

"You're goin' to fix my daughters, Mister Holten, an' I'll be much obliged for it, before this . . . playactin' as they call it . . . becomes all they know. They gotta want husbands. Gotta know a man 'twixt their legs. Out here, with just their father to look at, their natural closeness has grown into something . . . unusual."

Eli shot another look to Samantha at his feet. Her tongue snuck out of the corner of her petite mouth as she timidly reached to the opening of his buckskin trousers.

"They're children!" Eli shouted in shocked protest.

"They're nearly sixteen years old an' diddlin' with each other fer more'n five of those," Duddles answered in a choked voice. "That's more than a might bit precocious by my lights. It's time for them to. . ." her voice trailed off.

Eagle Butte would be attacked soon, Eli thought. Unless he ran to save it. "Ma'am," Eli began to explain. "There's a large number of desperados headed for Eagle Butte. If I don't get there before them, they're gonna kill the marshal and who knows all else."

"You'll have plenty of time for that," Susan countered, perhaps not comprehending what the scout said, her eyes slightly glazed with moisture. "Damn, Holten. You'd think I was geldin' ya. You can't tell me my daughters ain't appeallin'. I'm not that blinded by my mother's eyes."

Samantha squealed with delight as she recklessly plunged her hand inside the scout's tightly stretched buckskins and her cool, damp fingers circled the thick base of his rigid organ. Sybil edged forward in anticipa-

139

tion. Her eyes fixed on the engorged flesh lance that her sister drew from within the leather trousers.

"Mama!" Samantha cried and pulled back, a wondering expression akin to fear suddenly filling her face at the size of the throbbing object in her hand. Susan studied the swaying maleness with a cooler eye, although admiration pursed her lips.

"You mean you're givin' me your daughters to fuck, then? Is that it?" Eli asked brutally. He made a point to describe what she seemed to imply in the crudest words in hopes she might change her mind and free him.

"Oh, Mama! It's beautiful," Samantha cried with childish delight as she pressed her silky cheek against the deep red tip of Holten's penis and stroked it gently.

"T-that's exactly what I mean," Susan managed to gasp out. "You gonna do it?" She lowered the barrels of the shotgun.

Holten noted the slight hesitation, the hint of a quaver in her voice and pressed his advantage in swift invention. "I'm a real man, Mrs. Duddles," he said honestly. Then he looked her straight in the eye, ready to pull his big bluff. "Once I start, I'll keep goin' 'til I'm sated and the girls cry for mercy. If they aren't enough for me, I'll turn to you for pleasurin', whether your husband shows or not. It could get pretty ugly if Mister Duddles were to find me with his daughters . . . or a foot deep in his wife."

"He'll be gone another four, five days," the mother answered coolly. "You don't have to worry about him bustin' in before we . . . uh, you three get all you want of each other. You don't be afraid, either, Samantha," she went on as she leaned toward her kneeling daughter and clucked maternally. She sat the shotgun aside, muzzle leaning on the front wall of a stall.

"Touch it again," Susan instructed her daughter. "That's it. Yes . . . stroke it . . . faster . . . like that . . . good girl. Isn't that better than doin' it with your sister?"

Then Holten made his move.

With a rapid drop at his knees and a quick grab, he filled his right fist with the butt of his Remington and pulled it free of the sagging holster. The hammer ratcheted back and he steadied the black hole of the muzzle on Maw Duddles' ample chest. His heart pounded, not entirely from the urgency and danger of his actions. His traitorous body had begun to respond with wave after wave of delightful sensation to the inexpert, but sincere, ministrations of little Samantha.

"Stop that," he commanded her a bit more sharply than his tingling body wanted him to. "Your daughters may have a game of their own they like to play, but this one you thought up is over, Mrs. Duddles."

"Suck it, Samantha!" an apparently unperturbed Susan Duddles commanded. "Take that big thing in your mouth and suck it good. No man can resist that."

Roughly Eli stepped away from the amorous twin. Her sister scurried forward and reached for his reddened and pulsating flesh, eyes alight with the same fire of longing and hunger. Eli gently shoved her aside while his body railed at him for refusing such a bountiful gift.

"Fix me something to eat, Mrs. Duddles. Ham, some fatback or a steak and half dozen eggs. Milk if you've got it. Biscuits an' gravy. Some fresh onions from that garden. Do it quick. The girls. . .the, uh, girls can clean and dress my wounds while you're about it."

Susan Duddles looked long and hard at the wicked

hole in the Remington's muzzle end and sighed with resignation. "Maybe next time, Mr. Holten?"

Eli relaxed enough to smile. "*Definitely* next time, Mrs. Duddles, provided my duties bring me this way."

"You're a gentleman, Mrs. Holten, even if you do work for the army." Susan hurried from the barn to prepare a meal. Holten reholstered his revolver and, suddenly weaker than any time since his struggle to reach Big Wolf's village, sat down on the hay.

Sybil, with slight help from the scout, removed his buckskin shirt while Samantha tended to the remainder of his clothes. While the one twin hurried after hot water and cloths to make bandage and bindings, Samantha proved herself to be of singleminded purpose when it came to obeying her mother's wishes.

Swiftly she lowered her head over the turgid, vibrating shaft that poked skyward from Holten's loins and covered as much of it as she could with her sweet mouth and mobile lips. Shocks of incredible pleasure flashed through the scout's weary body and he surrendered to the inevitable while the first delicious odors of the meal being prepared came to his quivering notrils.

"I . . . I could feel what you were doin', Samantha," Sybil panted when she returned. "It . . . was . . . wonderful. Let's hurry and get him fixed up, then I can do it, too."

Samantha giggled as she changed her position, throwing her naked thighs astraddle of the supine scout's hips and lowering her dripping cavity toward the fiery plug she knew would fill it just so perfectly.

"An' this, too, sweet sister," Samantha cried in delirious joy.

Still fired with the necessity of his urgent mission. Eli

142

Holten wondered how much time it would take for his wounds to be tended and to finish his meal so he could ride on to warn Eagle Butte. A large, upthrusting part of him hoped it would take a long, long while.

The wind, which had blown steadily against the point of Eli Holten's right shoulder shifted suddenly and blasted at him from out of the north. In a matter of five minutes the temperature plummeted by thirty degrees. Small clouds, which had seemed insignificant before, now gathered into a dense gray-black mass that obscured the sky and blotted out the sun. Eli's mind had been filled with warm thoughts of the eager twins and their joyful defloration and his body had tingled with remembered delights.

Now the warmth had fled and his flesh prickled with cold instead of passion. In another ten minutes snow began to fall.

Holten quickly discerned that this was no mere early sample of winter. A howling gale replaced the ragged icy blast from the north and the large, wet, white flakes fell in such profusion that he soon became unable to see more than a dozen feet in front of his horse's nose. On the fury raged.

At first the fat puffs melted on contact with the ground. Within a half-hour, a thick carpet of white covered the ground and direction lost all meaning. Determined to outdistance the Barlow gang and warn Eagle Butte, Holten forced himself onward. Frigid blasts assaulted him from the north and a whirlwind of snow blinded man and horse. Reeling from the intensity of the blizzard, the scout struggled forward in a world empty of all save him and the storm. He paused only long enough to shrug into the single warm coat he located in the dead gunhawk's rig, a flannel-lined wool jacket, over which he placed a gummy black rain slicker. Head bent, he forced his mount ahead, against knee-deep drifts.

Soon the level stretches had reached the same depth, with drifts chest deep. The temperature arrowed downward again and Holten felt numbness spreading through his arms from exposed fingers and upward from his unprotected feet. His face had become set, encased in crusted snow and ice and blue lips had closed tightly over his teeth. His senses seemed to abandon him for a while and all he could think of was sleep. How nice and peaceful it would be to sleep for long hours. On the horse plodded.

Holten swayed in his saddle and jerked only partially awake.

On the level, the powdery white demon had risen to nearly the animal's chest. With great effort it lunged forward, a thick wake curling from behind it. The man on its back continued to shiver and mutter unintelligible words to himself. At last he swayed recklessly to the right and fell into the deep accumulation of frigid flakes. Despite his body's surrender, Holten tightly grasped the reins in his left hand.

Chapter Twelve

A peaceful silence surrounded the inert form of the scout. Holten strained to remain conscious and wondered at the strange sense of warmth he found in the deep snow that enveloped him. Gradually, despite his efforts, his body began to relax and his mind drifted over the past to forgotten scenes of his youth.

Abandoned on the prairie in the summer of his fifteenth year, Eli had been found by a small hunting party of Sioux. They had taken the youth to their village and there he had been adopted by the nominal chief of the band, Two Horns, who had recently lost a son to the whiteman's curse, smallpox. While he lived with the Oglala, they raised him like one of their own. Among the Sioux, as was the case with all the tribes of the plains, when a boy reached puberty, he sought his purpose in life, his future, and his secret name by going off to a secluded spot and waiting for a Helper to come and be his guide to the mysteries of the Spirit World.

Eli, although well past puberty, went in his turn with two Oglala boys of thirteen to the rugged, densely forested peaks of the *pahasapa,* the Black Hills, sacred place of the Sioux and many other tribes. First the youngsters built a small brush lodge and took sweatbaths to cleanse their souls as well as their bodies. They rubbed sweet-smelling herbs on their naked bodies before beginning their quest. Owls hooted under the gathering stars when Eli and the other boys climbed their separate peaks to seek out their Helpers, Spirit Persons who would come to them to guide their dreams.

On that first night, Holten made his bed of sweet sage and ground cedar slightly below the top of the mountain he'd climbed. He shivered in the chill mountain night air, lacking even moccasins to cover his feet. For three days he walked in circles, broiled by the sun and unable to gain the summit. He ate no food and drank no water, waiting for the Helpers to come. When he stopped and slept, he pointed his feet to the east. On the fourth day he'd sworn he would either walk on that peak or die. Again he failed.

At midnight on the fourth night, the young Eli heard a voice say softly, "Come this way."

He turned and saw in the east a soft, white, indistinguishable form dancing at the top of the peak. Holten, though he had been weak for the last two days, had no trouble climbing to the pinnacle of the mountain.

When he reached the top, he could see the Person as a tall, lean white bear that wore a loincloth like a warrior and had bare legs like a man. The Spirit Person held a bow string in one hand and a woman's burden-bearing brow strap in the other. He offered both to Eli with equal eagerness. With lightening speed, the youthful Holten reached out and grabbed the bow string.

Then the bear showed him many things that he did not fully understand. The Helper walked him through blue uniforms hanging neatly on trees and introduced him to the wolves and eagles, mighty predators who tracked and scouted for their food. The bear told Holten many things to look for in his life.

"You are an Oglala boy . . . yet you are not," the bear had said. "You either stand torn by the difference or you hold on to it. If you grasp it tightly, it will serve you always."

Eli woke much later, a whole day after he had started the dream-walk, and returned to the village. There he sought out the medicine man to have his vision interpreted. The wise old shamen didn't explain much of the dream to Holten, but from that day on, the uncles and other sons of Two Horns, his adopted father, stressed teaching him how to scout. Before long he could find his way and track others in the worst of weather or the darkest of night. They named him Tall Bear, because of his Spirit Helper.

Now, Eli dreamed again, only vaguely feeling the horse tugging at the reins in his left hand. An eerie sound stirred Eli's buried form.

The scout looked up and saw the white bear, his Spirit Helper, stood a short distance off, snow swirling by, though the bear didn't seem to notice.

"Come, Tall Bear," his Helper commanded.

Eli rose with no trouble and let go of the horse. He feared nothing, not the frigid blasts of wind-driven snow nor losing his mounts.

The Spirit Person turned and walked to the north, toward a stand of trees that Eli hadn't seen before. As winds whipped cold wet flakes into the scout's eyes, his Helper stopped and waited for him to catch up.

Holten could see something hanging from the trees. He could not make it out, the falling white flakes obscuring his view. The bear pointed away from the branches at the base of one of the pines.

A weasel huddled there, shivering in the cold. Eli

wondered why the animal didn't run to its hole. Then he saw that its front legs wrapped around the tree. On the other side, its paws were held fast in a trap. A book, its insides cut out, lay open next to the trap. The weasel turned its eyes up to Eli and looked imploringly.

"A cunning animal, the weasel, and a creature that has a place in this world. It will die, despite its cunning," the white bear noted dispassionately. "Unless someone comes and cuts it loose."

"Will I not die shortly as well?" Eli asked. "I am in the snow and so weak I can't get to the saddle."

"You will not die, though you have cheated death so many times you should not complain if it were so," the Helper answered. "It is your cunning that keeps you alive. It is your honesty and friends that give you luck that will save you this time. It is your holding on to both sides of your nature, Oglala and white, that will make you conquer the enemy you seek, though there is much suffering ahead before you make your enemy dance in the sky."

Eli bent to free the weasel and heard something above him. The small creature disappeared in a puff of smoke. Eli looked up and saw boots swinging back and forth and rope creaking like some unoiled door. Then the boots turned to moccasins with bare legs attached to them. The scout followed the legs up to a bare-chested warrior. Squinting, Eli saw the features of Big Wolf, who looked vaguely disgusted.

"Can Tall Bear hear me?" the warrior asked.

"I hear you, Big Wolf," Holten replied and knew the dream had ended. He lay as he had, beside the patient gray, buried in the snow.

"I have come to return your fine horse and to get my

148

ponies back. I expected to see a scalp hanging from your belt. Instead, I see you have lost my animals."

"I regret losing your horses," Eli answered honestly. "I had no choice."

"It is not good that I keep finding Tall Bear on the ground," the Oglala war chief announced sternly. Holten felt a spasm of irritation ripple through his belly.

"Go away then," the scout returned as best he could. "If the sight of me offends you, leave me here. I have fought sixteen men when I thought I faced only one. I have counted *coup* on three of them. I have no fear of dying, nor do I have a single wound that I didn't earn honorably. If this is not true, then leave me to die."

Big Wolf's face remained stern and impassive, yet his words were conciliatory. "I did not accuse you of lying, my friend, and now I *must* take you to the sacred hoop and hear your whole story, so that we may mention your name in council lodges and perhaps even sing a song about you."

The scout struggled to a sitting position. The freak storm had stopped. His body heat had begun to melt the snow, soaking into his clothing, and the frigid wind chilled him until he knew how the dead felt.

"I must live, Big Wolf," Holten looked up at the brave. "My friends are in danger at Eagle Butte and I must ride there quickly."

"Come," Big Wolf said, motioning at the scout with his chin. Two braves slid off their mounts and went to help Eli. "We will let Thunder Woman look at you."

Farther northwest, out of the path of the freak blizzard, Ezekiel Smith sang out loud to the Lord on His day. The preacher's bosom swelled with the love he had for his God, and his face warmed with the sun and his faith. He sang *Onward, Christian Soldiers,* his favorite hymn, until any other person would have lost Christian patience and shot him. Only his mount and the pack-mules he hauled behind him could hear the reverend's caterwauling, though, and they didn't seem to mind. After the singing, Smith pulled his Bible from a saddlebag and set to reading.

Nathan Barlow studied the trail ahead, even though two point men rode far out, reconnoitering their route. The vengeful rustler didn't intend to accidentally run into an army patrol. From what he could see, they'd be the only ones that could stop him. He didn't fear Indians or settlers. He had the men to handle either.

One of the point riders galloped hard and fast back to the main body. "Rider out ahead, Mister Barlow," the hired gun shouted out before he had even stopped.

Jed Barlow and Bart Blackwell edged their horses closer to hear the report. The younger Barlow gave Bart a dirty look, but Blackwell didn't seem to notice.

"What's it look like?" Nathan asked.

"Looks like a preacher, reading his Bible and all," the rider said with a chuckle. He lost his smile and greed tainted his features. "He's got a pack-horse that can barely walk it's so loaded."

"Gonna knock him off, Mister Barlow?" Blackwell eagerly inquired.

"Boy," Nathan growled ominously as he started peeling the young drifter's face skin off with his fiery eyes. "Today is the Lord's day, iffin you've forgot. I'm not about to kill or rob a man of the cloth today, or anyone else for that matter."

"Sorta strange he ain't in church with his people to-day, ain't it, Nate?" Jed asked, rolling a cigarette and lighting it.

"It's curious," the older Barlow allowed. He thought a moment, then turned to the out-rider again.

"Where's he headed?"

"Right toward us, the man answered. "Be here in two, three hours."

That seemed to satisfy Nate. "When he gets here, we'll find out what he's all about."

Shelter through the remainder of the night under a hastily erected windbrake where Big Wolf and his party had weathered out the storm, a warm meal, and a chance to dry his clothes solved most of Eli's needs. The main Oglala camp had moved further south and it only took half a day to get there. In that time, Holten told the war cheif about the four young Cheyenne and the large number of killers marching on Eagle Butte.

"It is not our concern when whitemen kill whitemen," Big Wolf commented off-handedly after considering Eli's words. "The Cheyenne, though, are our brothers. They are not like the Crow, or the Shoshone at the Rose Bud. They have always been our friends. I will take this up at the council fire and see if we might help you."

In this, Eli took hope. It would be worth the delay if he could get the mighty Sioux to stop the bandits. The scout spent the rest of the trip back to the Oglala village worrying about Zeke Smith.

The minister, his heart afire with his faith, remained absorbed in the words in his book as his horse chose its own path. So enraptured was the preacher, he didn't see the approaching riders until Nathan Barlow called out from six feet away.

"Morning, Reverend," he greeted politely.

Zeke looked up from his book, his mind still in the state of bliss his religion gave him. He smiled at the large number of riders.

"Well, howdy," his voice boomed from his horse pulpit. He paused to stand in his stirrups and study the body of men. "Blessed be the name of the Lord. My name's Reverend Ezekiel Smith."

"Mine's Nathan, Reverend Smith," Barlow answered with a smile.

"A mighty warrior of the Lord. So many of you," the minister added, then he came to a fatal conclusion. "You boys a posse?"

"We're in search of justice, Reverend," the leader of the rustlers answered coldly, "if that's what you mean."

In the bosom of God's warmth, Smith didn't notice the subtle, chilling, difference. He raised a hand in benediction and threw back his head.

"Halleluiah!" he cried. " 'Do me justice, O God, and fight my fight against the faithless people; from the deceitful and impious man, rescue me.' "

"Amen," Nathan answered, his voice ashiver with fervor. Then he leaned on his saddle horn and stared into the preacherman's eyes. "Long way from a church on the Sabbath."

"And to be with my people today would be good for my soul," Zeke answered. "Alas, I am in the service of God here, too. I'm pursuing a fine man of righteousness, who seeks to bring to justice a young scalawag that took part in a robbery and murder in our humble town."

Blackwell shifted in his seat nervously and studied Barlow's eyes as Nathan tested the mettle of the minister.

"You wouldn't be from Eagle Butte, would you, Reverend?"

"Why, indeed I am," Zeke replied enthusiatically. "I'm running supplies to our one-man posse, Eli Holten. Have you seen him?"

Nathan Barlow smiled, a mountain lion comtemplating a tender young lamb.

"You know, Reverend Smith, I believe that God sent you to me."

Eli felt much better physically, but the council was making him ill.

The pipe had been passed and Big Wolf had said his piece. He urged the warriors in camp to go in pursuit of the Barlow Gang and stop it before it reached Eagle Butte. His opinion met a cold response.

"If Tall Bear speaks the truth, then there is no hope to stop these whitemen," one wizened old grandfather announced. "They are many, with better guns than we have. There are only six young warriors in this camp, against more than ten of them."

"Thirteen men," Eli offered. "Including the man I sought."

"We should wait until they come back this way," a younger brave offered. "What do we care if they should wipe out the whiteman's village? Perhaps there will be less of them when they they go this way again and we will have gathered more warriors from other villages to lay in wait for them."

The men of the council began to argue whether to wait to attack or not fight at all. Big Wolf spoke for a moment, asking the gathered men to consider the dead Cheyenne, but the grandfather answered him paternally.

"Patience is a virtue which perhaps Big Wolf should tender," the wise old man advised. "We could not hope to stop them without more help."

Eli realized no one but Big Wolf even considered the thought of stopping Barlow and his men before they reached Eagle Butte. The others had a point he hadn't considered. The winter camps were small, of necessity, and it would take time to gather enough men to take a group like the Barlow Gang. Holten's mind set to work on other plans even as the council continued. The scout thought about heading for Fort Rawlins and getting the army to send out a company, but that would take too much time. He still had to get to Eagle Butte to warn them, and now he'd wasted precious time talking with the Oglala.

Abe Suttler, a good man with a six-shooter and also known for his brawling abilities, took the lead in questioning the minister. He landed a big beefy fist in Smith's abdomen and the reverend's lungs emptied in a whoosh.

"How many men in Eagle Butte, Reverend?" Nathan asked from the saddle as Suttler slapped Zeke into a pine.

"I don't know," he wheezed.

"If anybody'd know, the minister of a town would, " Jed countered.

"What about my brother?" Bart Blackwell interjected. "What have they done with him?"

"They're gonna try him real quick," Zeke answered instantly, glad to get off the other subject.

"Reverend," Nathan started, straightening himself in the saddle and studying the pine branches above him. "We took care of Eli Holten, in the name of righteous vengeance. 'Vengeance is mine,' the Good Book says. And on him that has done me dirt, I have taken thus."

"Actually," Smith managed though swelling lips, "it's 'Vengeance is mine, sayeth the Lord.' "

Nathan glowered at the minister until the pummeled Bible pusher fidgeted. "Well, after all, it's my job to read the Bible. I ought to know how it goes," Smith elaborated.

"What're we goona do with him, Nathan?" Jed asked.

"I don't know about the rest of you," Slim Cranston leered at their young prisoner, "but I'm feelin' a might horny. Maybe we oughta do like we did in Leavenworth when they'd bring in tender young deserter that caught our fancy."

"How dare you suggest such a disgusting and blasphemous thing on the Lord's day!" Nathan boomed at Cranston, who blanched at his boss' anger.

"Well, *what are* we going to do with him, Nate?" Jed repeated, sucking deeply on his cigarette.

"We will not kill a man of the cloth," Nathan answered forcefully. "We will deliver him unto God and let the Lord decide what is to be done."

Thunder Woman, pouting prettily at the scout, gave him a pouch of herbs and a hot meal. Her medicine warmed him inside and out. It was getting late, but Eli knew he'd wasted most of the day coming to the camp to talk with the leaders of the village. He had to overtake Barlow and get to Eagle Butte before the rustlers and desperados did.

Big Wolf joined him at the edge of camp, ready to ride. "I will go with you, Tall Bear," the war chief spoke grimly. "You are a friend and I wish to help."

"You have been a good friend, Big Wolf," Eli answered, resting a hand on the Oglala's shoulder. "But the council decided not to follow me and I fear it will put you in bad with them. I do not wish you to be frowned on by the council. I will go alone. If you could, though, keep a watchful eye open for my friend, the Black Robe. He was supposed to follow me but I have not seen him for many days now."

"If he is south of here," Big Wolf assured him, "I will find him, though he might have been caught in the blizzard and died. If he is north of here, you keep your eyes open, for your might pass him on your way back to the whiteman's town."

"Either way, I'll need the ammunition he is carrying," Holten observed. "There's going to be a powerful fight in Eagle Butte."

Chapter Thirteen

For the first time in nearly a week, Marshal Peters sat up in bed. The townsfolk patiently waited their turn to visit outside the boarding house. Mrs. O'Flannery, the pink-cheeked large-girthed widow lady who owned the establishment, laid down the law on how guests to her home and business accounted for themselves.

"No swearing," she warned with a big wooden ladle in her beefy Irish hands. "No carousing and *no* drinking."

There they sat; the blacksmith, the mercantile owner, the soiled doves of the Thunder Saloon, the bank teller, and nearly everyone else in town, sooner or later, all waiting patiently in line, some on the divan in the parlor, most outside where the cold wind whipped up the single street of Eagle Butte, silent and proper in their Sunday best.

Marshal Peters greted each one individually, scowling at the town drunk who weaved in, as near to sober as the time spent in front of the boarding house allowed. Peters blustered at the teller, a middle-aged, mild, meek Easterner who had come out to the Wild West dreaming of glory and quick justice with a Colt and who idolized the cool, calm manner of the town marshal. Finally, Peters talked serious business with the saloon owner.

"Has anyone gone looking for Holten and the Reverend?" Peters inquired, a slight hint of impatience in his voice.

"A couple of the boys have ridden as far as the Cheyenne, Marshal," Jason Scruggs, the tavern keeper, answered. His cheeks flamed with embarrassment that more had not been done. "But they haven't seen hide nor hair of Holten, Blackwell, of Reverend Smith."

"Holten should've gotten that scalawag in before we tried Blackwell's brother," Peters snapped, angered at himself as much as the man who had his New York bowler in his hand. "Something's gone wrong." He turned his complete attention to the barkeep.

"I want you to get the town ready for an attack."

The neatly waxed handle bar moustache on the face of the saloon owner twitched with surprise and consternation. "From whom, Marshal?"

"The other Blackwell and his friends . . . or the Barlow gang," Peters answered coldly. "And, no, I'm not suffering a relapse."

Eli settled the frail minister down on a blanket and cursed under his breath. Chills wracked the preacher's body and a blue tinge ringed his lips.

"It's too early to stop," Zeke protested.

"We've traveled a good distance today," Holten observed.

"The Barlows have traveled more," the reverend countered, his breath wheezed out from the very depths of his soul. A liquid rattle from his lungs accompanied his efforts.

"The horses are spent," Eli suggested. How long had they been pursuing the Barlows? Four days?

Or was it five?

"Damnit, Eli," the minister cursed. "It's the whole town of Eagle Butte those boys are hunting. They as much as told me that."

"I know that's the way of it," Eli placated. "But I can't leave you like this. You're on the edge of pneumonia. And besides, we've been gainin' on them."

"Not quickly enough, Eli," Zeke pressed. "I swear to you, I'll be all right. I made it through the war . . . I can make it here, too. I'm not new to such problems of surviving. You think I'm just some Bible-pounding preacher, but I served in Sherman's army and I'm not an Eastern weakling who needs to be coddled."

"I'm not leaving you," the scout declared flatly, bringing the discussion to an end. He set about making the last meal of the day. As he did, he reflected on their situation.

Standing against that pine had proved more draining to Reverend Smith than he expected, Holten thought. But then, more than five hours lashed to a tree in one's stocking feet, no food nor water, in sinking temperatures . . . well, Smith must be a lot frailer now than he'd been in Sherman's march to the sea.

"Zeke?" Eli asked as he set a sulphur-sputtering lucifer to kindling. "How in hell did a soldier in the Union Army ever see fit to become a preacher? Were you a chaplain?"

"It was in the very hell you swear by that I found God," Smith told him gently. "And no, I wasn't a chaplain. You see, Eli, my friend, some men need to see in order to believe. They need something to have faith in. I needed to believe." The minister fell back on his elbows. His strength ebbed and flowed like ripples on the Missouri.

An ashen color hung on his cheeks, though Eli had kept him warm and dry for all these long days.

"I believed we needed to keep our fellow Americans in this great Union, by force if necessary. I saw the truth of Mister Lincoln's words. I felt the holy power that let our forces stand victorious against better fighting men than we were."

Smith turned toward the suddenly gaining gloom of the fall night. His eyes lost the religious fervor that usually filled them and made them dance. The gray orbs seemed to grow sickly with his thoughts.

"Then we marched through Georgia to the sea behind Sherman. Under orders I burned and pillaged those same fellow Americans I wanted to keep to the bosom of the Union. I saw them hanged for no more offense than not bowing and scraping to an arrogant Union officer. Saw them stripped of all they possessed and left destitute, despite the President's words. I witnessed black men in the uniform of the Confederacy fighting of their own free will to stop us.

"Then . . . then that evil political cabal murdered the South's only hope of justice, there in Ford's Theatre." A chill seemed to settle in Zeke's body. He dug into his blanket. "After what I saw there in the heart of Georgia, done in the name of 'justice' I swore I'd never put my faith in earth-bound trappings, but seek the true *justice* of Our Lord."

Eli forestalled his reply as he poked the reluctant fire further into life. A tightness had formed in his chest and Zeke's words brought a silence that left both men alone with their conscience.

"We may not make it," Eli finally said. "Even if I left you right now, we wouldn't make it, not at the speed Barlow's moving."

"I know," Smith agreed.

Barlow's first real break came the day after the motley group of thieves and hired guns left Reverend Smith tied to the tree.

"God is with us," Nathan had intoned over the herd of horses he admired from a rise.

Thirty handsome animals grazed in a field next to a soddy. The rustlers rode down to the earthen cabin and discovered a single young wrangler, wearing a large, floppy sombero and jangling spurs in the sunlight as he swaggered out of his shelter.

"Howdy," he greeted the large band of riders. Experience had taught him to be cautious. Though he held the Winchester Henry casually, his finger was curled around the trigger and his thumb rested on the hammer, ready to draw it back.

"Howdy to you," Jed answered. Then he drew his revolver and blew a hole through the boy's belly that left the hired hand screaming in pain.

"Round up those critters," Nathan ordered. "Each of you take a fresh mount and a reserve. Kill any extra stock."

"That seems awful wasteful," Cooper rebuked.

"If anybody's following us, I don't want 'em to get fresh horses," Nate replied.

The bandits picked out the twelve finest horses in the field and cut them out of the herd, then selected a dozen more for the remuda. That task completed, with the giddy thrill of wanton destruction, they opened fire on the other animals in the field until they reduced the herd to fly food. Within seconds, the buzzing sound of the voracious insects filled the air behind the Barlow gang.

The second bit of Barlow's good fortune came to him without his knowledge.

The horse Zeke rode stuck its foot into a gopher hole. Eli winced with the crunching sound that crackled in his ears as he rode a few yards ahead of the holy man, split seconds before the minister's mount let go an ear-splitting scream of agony.

Smith tumbled off the beast, smashed to the hard ground and battered his already weakened body.

Eli leveled his Remington to the ear of the suffering animal. The report of its merciful dispatch sent shudders through the shaken preacher.

"Thank God for the extra horse, Reverend," Holten offered in an attempt to console the minister. They rearranged the saddle and rode on.

The pair came on the soddy, the murdered wrangler, and slaughtered horses near sundown. The scout knew what it all meant and Smith had fairly good idea. Wrapped in their silent feelings, neither one expressed how much the scene of butchery sickened them.

Despite these two benefits to Barlow's trip, the pursuing men closed the gap to less than a day behind the brigands. They would come on Barlow's previous day's camps before midday, inspect the cold fires and try to learn what they could about the gang's condition, strength, and security measures.

Twice Eli rode out to find fresh game to feed himself

and Smith and this wasted more time. The large number of men in Barlow's group, though, tended to slow the rustlers down.

Finally, the Barlows crossed the Cheyenne River, at a point that put Eagle Butte due north.

"Eagle Butte is no more than a day and a half's ride from here," Nathan announced. "Cooper, pick the men I wanted to go into that rancid town and send them ahead. The rest of us are gonna move as close to invisible as possible. We're gonna sleep during the day and ride quietly at night. From now on it's a cold camp until we're done with Eagle Butte."

Eli and Zeke crossed the Cheyenne River at midday. Thirty miles to the east lay Eagle Butte. Holten bent over the last remnants of a fire circle.

The scout gave the Barlows a good day, give or take a night, ahead of them. The number of horses told him what he'd suspected all along. With his fresh mounts, Barlow would now be on the outskirts of the unsuspecting town.

Inside the Thunder Saloon, the men of Eagle Butte sat staring at their beers. For a long while none spoke and the piano remained silent.

He's crazy," Luke the blacksmith finally proclaimed. "There ain't no one headed this way."

"If there was, they wouldn't stand a chance," the bartender, Opey Scruggs, brother of the owner, added. "There wasn't but four, five men in the Barlow gang an' that Blackwell feller was alone. What are any of them gonna do? Storm the town like Injuns?"

I think we oughta put someone armed in the store next to the safe," the owner of the Mercantile suggested. "If they did ride in, that's what they'd be after."

"The telegram says the Barlow bunch is headed for Coffeville, Kansas," Luke, a barrel-chested man countered. "There ain't no one to fend off."

At that moment, two bedraggled strangers came loudly through the swinging doors of the saloon. Several ladies smiled prettily at them and the newcomers leered back, sizing the harlots up. But they made no offer.

"Howdy, strangers," Opey greeted. "What'll it be?"

"Beer," the taller of the pair ordered.

"I sure could stand a whiskey," the second man announced wistfully. At a glower from his companion, he hastily changed his order. "Uh . . . make it a beer."

"Where you boys ridin' from?" Luke asked as he sidled up to them.

The two men looked at each other, then back at the blacksmith. "Who wants to know?" the taller one demanded.

"My name's Luke," the big man replied with a smile. "I work the metal in these parts."

"I'm Leroy McDade," the tall one introduced himself. He forced a meaningless smile to his face, wiped his hand on his whipcord trousers and offered it to the blacksmith. "This here's Tim Swanson, my partner. We're looking to settle in these parts. We have a way with horses, so I better be treatin' you right, huh, Smithy?"

Luke grinned and nodded, then walked over to the table where his confederates sat. "Straight talkers," Luke announced to the other men, not noticing the weak handshake he received from the two. "I like that." He seated himself and turned back to the unknown pair.

"The reason I ask is, our marshal got shot up a few weeks ago, still a little weak. Bedridden, matter o' fact. He thinks some real bad hombres are comin' in from Kansas and the town should be ready for a fight."

"Luke," Opey growled at the blacksmith under his breath. The other townies fidgeted angrily. The blacksmith would converse with the Devil if the Fallen Angel offered a sympathetic ear.

"I, ah, was just wondering if you boys were coming from that direction and if you saw anything on the way?" Luke finished in a weak attempt to cover his previous indiscretion, vaguely aware the rest of the patrons had turned cold faces to him.

"Well, yeah. We came up the Missouri on a steamboat," Leroy responded and tried his best to look sincere. "Didn't see nobody for days. Then we came across this reverend with another fellow . . . Holten, he said his name was. Works for the army?"

"Rode with them a spell after they'd caught up with some bank robber from what we could make of it," Swanson added in, reinforcing the yarn. He shook his head and looked perplexed. "Never saw a lynchin' by a preacher before. He even prayed mighty powerful 'fore he tied the knot. That how it's done in these parts?"

Luke slapped rock-hard hands together in glee. "There. You see?" he proclaimed triumphantly. "Holten caught up with the bastard."

"If they done hanged Blackwell," an old man in the corner beside the piano observed, "how come they ain't back here yet?"

"They was talkin' to some Indian braves, last we saw of them," Leroy offered. "We rode on ahead."

"Then they're right behind you?" Opey pressed.

"Last we saw of them, they was talkin' with some Injuns," Tim repeated. "We don't know where they are."

"Not to worry," Luke insisted. "They'll be along d'rectly."

Leroy and Tim had been chosen by Cooper because they'd never been to the Black Hills area and couldn't be recognized. Also for their ability to strike up a conversation and think on their feet. Shortly, on the pretext of looking for some good land to stake out a homestead, they knew every inch of the town, including the location of the bank vault, where the local gunsmith had his shop, and most important, where Orsen Peters recuperated.

In the thickening tree cover along a deep, fast-flowing creek, Zeke Smith brought his horse to a stop, crawled off and pulled his carbine free of its scabbard. He removed his canteen and bedroll from the saddle skirt and hitched them over his shoulder. Then he walked forward and handed the reins to an astonished Holten.

"Ride like the Devil was after you and get to Eagle Butte," Zeke ordered.

"Haven't we talked about this before?" Eli shot back.

"I can walk back to town from here," the minister pointed out. "Take the horse and spend it out until you're in Eagle Butte. There's no time to argue. We've closed the gap and if you'd just press the animals a bit, you could get there in time."

"I don't know, Reverend . . ." Eli started.

"I do." Zeke cut the scout short. "I'm safe now. We've

paced them all the way here. You might be able to beat them to town. Or at least get there in time to organize the folks and chase them out."

Holten looked at the reins in his hand, then back at the minister. He knew, deep down, that two tired, spent horses couldn't put him ahead of the Barlows, especially when he'd have to skirt around the gang to get into town. Even then, the people might simply not have time to prepare. But he had to try. Even with a hopeless cause.

"I'll go," he said simply.

"I will pray for you, Eli Holten, that you succeed," the preacher intoned.

"What will be, will be, Reverend," the scout countered philosophically. He turned due north and prodded the roan Morgan forward.

McDade and Swanson left town a few hours before dark. Most of the good available homestead land lay to the east. Still, they headed south until they hooked up with the Barlow gang, camped and hour out of town.

What did you find out?" Cooper demanded of his two men.

"Everything but the marshal's birthday," Swanson replied through a smug, cruel smile.

"Break camp," Barlow ordered. "Tonight we settle down on the rise outside Eagle Butte."

The twelve men in the group skirted homesteads and soddies until they reached a high rise that gave a clear overview of the town. In a cabin on the ridge they found an old trapper who'd settled there on the hill long before Eagle Butte existed.

"Howdy," the old-timer greeted warily as he eared back the hammer on his buffalo rifle. "Out a mite late, ain'tcha?"

"Evenin'," Nathan answered as he pulled his hat from his head and stepped close to the door where the woodsman stood, followed closely by his brother and Cooper. "My name's . . ."

"Nathan Barlow," the white-whiskered frontiersman responded, only at that moment recognizing the rustler.

Cooper threw the knife hidden in his sleeve with the speed of a thought. It smacked to its hilt in the bony breast of the trapper. The blade buried itself in the old man's heart. Nathan leapt forward and slammed his thumb in between the hammer and nipple at the instant the old-timer's gnarled finger, with the last conscious act of his body, pulled the trigger.

Barlow gritted his teeth as the heavy, spring-propelled hammer crushed down on the web of his hand. The rifle remained silent. It never had the chance to discharge and warn the town.

In the dark, Eli pressed forward. Exhaustion ached at his eyes and he knew he still had many hours of riding. The strength of Smith's mount gave out quickly and didn't seem to get better with the care Eli offered it. Sonny's flanks, chest, and neck were slathered with lather until finally Holten was forced to dismount and walk the two animals through the night.

Morning could only be a few hours away.

Chapter Fourteen

To the west, the sun had yet to illuminate the mountainous crests of the Black Hills. A cold north wind bit at the trees, hills, and raw wooden facades of Eagle Butte. Luke, the blacksmith, got to work early, kindling the fire in his forge, bringing the flames to a powerful heat. He had iron tires to shrink onto three wagon wheels. The order was due that morning and he'd barely started.

The stable hand stirred next. The horses in the livery had to be fed. Some were due for a grooming and there were several saddles to be mended.

Opey opened the saloon shortly after that and, by the time he had finished sweeping the boardwalk, the Mercantile shades had raised and the front door thrown wide to attract customers.

That's when Nathan Barlow lowered his field glasses for the last time.

"Mount up," he ordered and the twelve hardened predators swung into their saddles.

With military precision, the gang members broke into three groups. With the number of men he had and the element of surprise working in their favor, Barlow had no fear of splitting his forces. Swanson and McDade rode into town ahead of the attack, waved to several people they'd made themselves familiar with and rode directly to the gunsmith's shop. A green roller shade still blocked the glass panel of the door and a small "CLOSED" sign dangled from a string across its middle.

Cooper led four of his men and Harry Lemley, a Barlow boy, around to the east and came up from a gully that, except for the last hundred yards, hid their approach.

Nathan, Jed, Art Hawkins, John Hay, and Harlan Bowes charged into town, leaving Bart Blackwell to watch the extra horses. They reached Main Street right after the two friendly strangers smashed down the door to the gun shop and, once having secured the weapons there, opened up from inside on the streets of Eagle Butte.

Cooper and his men shot at the outhouses that dotted the backyards of the residential section, wounding more than one able-bodied man, caught literally with their pants down.

Pure bedlam fell on the suddenly awakened townsfolk. The gunsmith stumbled in from the back of the shop where he slept, to get shot in the thigh for his troubles. Jason Scruggs and his brother Opey dashed to the windows of their establishment, guns in hand, only to get pinned down from solid fire that shattered the checkered green-and-red paint-decorated windows and pockholed the inner wooden walls.

Women screamed as they sought refuge from the hard-pressed attack. Children cried and ran about in mortal terror while Nathan rode right to the open doors of the Mercantile, up under the eaves and into the store, pistols blazing in both hands. His tactic pinned down the owner and the timid bank teller.

To Nathan's immense pleasure, the safe sat wide

open. Jed and Art rushed in after him and grabbed up returned burlap sacks, into which they emptied the contents of the safe.

Cooper and his men charged into the saloon and chased Opey and Jason out the back. They didn't suffer a single wound, despite the efforts of the two surprised brothers.

"Take the windows upstairs," Cooper shouted to his men.

Shank O'Niel led the way up the steps. His Whitney-ville-Kennedy carbine projected in front of him as he kicked in a door.

A tall, lean girl sat upright in bed. Her curly locks cascaded over her shoulders as she held the covers to her neck. Their rich, coppery hue matched the color of the flocked wallpaper that decorated the narrow crib. It was the fear in her eyes, though, that stirred Shank's pecker to life. He leered at her and licked hungry lips.

Nathan left his brother, Hawkins, and John Hay to take care of the Mercantile and bank while Harlan Bowes, Chub Kennedy, and the eldest Barlow ran down the dusty street, covered by their compatriots on either side until they reached the boarding house.

"Saints preserve us!" Mrs. O'Flannery screamed as they burst in.

Several men, most still in their sleeping garments, stumbled down the steps. Like ducks in a shooting gallery, they got shot by the four vengeance-bound rustlers. The local card sharp, Winchester in hand, made it all the way to the bottom of the staircase before Barlow caught him in the left shoulder with a .44 slug. The bullet spun the gambler around, knocking a deck of loose cards from his breast pocket. Lady Luck went scattering out at the bottom of the stairs.

One man, a pots and pans drummer, threw up his hands in surrender and Kennedy let him have both barrels of a scattergun — a momento he had taken from the soddy they'd hit back in Kansas. The 00 buckshot blew the man's stomach out against the wall behind him on the stairs.

The Faro dealer recovered enough by then to swing his Winchester into line and blast off a round that burned a fiery trail along Chub Kennedy's rib cage. The blubbery hardcase let out a yowl that got drowned in the roar of Harlan Bowes' Remington.

The heavy .44 slug blew off the top of the card slick's head.

Two other men lay wounded on the staircase, unconscious though not mortally hit. As Chub Kennedy reloaded and covered the survivors, the other men charged up the steps, leaping over the prone bodies of their victims.

"Don't move, lady," Kennedy shouted at the Irish matron. "Or I'll kill you and tan your hide for a winter coat."

"I recognize that Armaugh lilt in yer voice an' I figure ye for a Donnahoe or a Kennedy. An' 'tiz a spalpeen bastard ye are," Mrs. O'Flannery told him coldly, controlled fury flaming in her steady eyes.

On the floor above, Nathan Barlow and Harlan Bowes cautiously inched into the hallway. They glanced at the blank faces of the doors.

The boarding house had no numbers on the rooms. Mrs. O'Flannery considered that to be like "runnin' a common hotel, or other places of ill-repute." McDade and Swanson, however, had found out it was the second door on the left that led to their target. Bowes took the far side of the door, Barlow the near.

"You want the honors?" Barlow smiled crookedly at Bowes.

"He ain't gonna be much if those fellows o' Cooper's heard right," Bowes said smiling back.

"He's recuperating," Barlow countered. "That could mean trouble."

"Hell, I'll kill him for you, Nate," Bowes laughed. He kicked the flimsy door open and led with his cocked revolver.

And came flying back out again, ahead of the report of a shotgun emptying both barrels through the doorway.

The blast picked the rustler up and threw him against the far wall. Blood splattered out in all directions as his perforated body struck in the clean and tidy hallway and ruined Mrs. O'Flannery's favorite wallpaper.

Barlow didn't hesitate. Bowes had not slid to the floor before Nate dashed into the room, his Remington .44 cocked.

Peters sat in bed with a shotgun in his lap, reaching for the big Smith & Wesson lying next to him.

Barlow fired and the slug caught Orsen's right shoulder. It knocked him to the headboard and away from his .44. Undaunted, Peters reached for a Winchester on the left side of the bed.

Barlow fired at point-blank range into Peters' breast. The black powder dumped gritty burns all over the marshal's chest, making a wide, spotty, circular pattern around the pulsing hole below his left nipple.

Peters belched blood up from his lungs. The spray jumped out past his sheet and splattered on the spread. Some splashed on Barlow, who jumped back as the marshal slid dead to one side of the bed.

Kennedy dashed into the room. "He got Harlan," Chub shouted.

"I tried to restrain him," Barlow answered grimly. "But he wanted first crack at Peters. It was the Lord's will."

The tubby rustler ran up to the bed and began to pistol whip the dead form of Orsen Peters. "Damn you!" Chub screamed. "Harlan was a friend of mine."

"Stop that!" Barlow snapped in a tone used on a naughty child. "We're gonna give Peters a taste of his own medicine." His voice shivered with emotion. He grabbed the twitching body of the marshal by one leg and started hauling the carcass toward the door. Kennedy grabbed the other and the two men quickly had Peters out on the street.

The townsfolk tried to return fire at the marauders who had stormed into Eagle Butte. The Barlow gang, however, could pepper any spot in the town from either the saloon, the gunsmithy, or the Mercantile. No one stood to lead the people since the volunteer would have been shot down. Then, when Barlow hauled the town marshal's body out onto the street, the people fell back into their homes and shops and cowered. For a good fifteen minutes, Eagle Butte fell silent and the Barlow gang owned the streets of the frontier town.

"Hey!" Shank O'Niel, one of Cooper's men, shouted from the second story balcony. He hauled a young painted lady behind him. "Look what I found."

"That's a damn good thing, boy!" Nate Barlow called up as he tied a rope around Peters' legs, then threw the other end of the lariat over a strut that stuck out of the bar's eaves.

"We've got about ten chippies up here," Slim Cranston added to the report. "Can we start fucking them?"

"Not now," Barlow ordered. With his brother's help, he hauled the marshal's bloody corpse up, leaving it dangling and bleeding on the dusty street. "Get them all together, round up enough horses so we can carry them along. That way we can pleasure ourselves at our leisure. Even the Lord rested on the seventh day."

The gunmen let out piercing Texas yells of delight and dashed back into the saloon to aid O'Niel and Cranston.

Eli heard the shooting from a short distance off. He tied the spare horse to a tree branch and mounted Sonny. Holten had walked most of the night, the animals showing little improvement after the treacherous push across the prairie. Sonny, though, looked somewhat refreshed. The scout had let the horses graze for a short time during the night and the Morgan seemed to perk up, as though he knew how important the mission was. Now Eli headed for the town, hoping to catch the Barlows when they weren't looking. As he rode, he reflected on the damage a few determined men could do to unsuspecting people.

Memory supplied him images of raids his adoptive Oglala band had made against villages of their enemies: the Crow, the *Palani,* and the *Pani.* They had been vicious, bloody affairs. Many on both sides received horrible wounds, though few actually died. In his turn, as the young initiate, Tall Bear, Holten had participated on three of these attacks.

In his remembered vision he saw again the contorted

face of a Pawnee boy, much younger than himself. The lad had raised up amid the ruins of his village to fire an arrow at Holten from only a dozen feet away. As Tall Bear of the Oglala, Eli had drummed his heels in his pony's ribs and leaped forward to drive his lance into the boy's guts.

The force of the impact had snapped off the shaft a foot from Holten's hand. The last sight of the *Pani* youngster had been of the child clutching the broken lance with both hands, his mouth open in a soundless scream.

The Oglala had burned every lodge in the encampment and went home with many horses and a few scalps. Although too late to drive off an attack by the Barlow gang, Eli still hoped to prevent a similar fate for Eagle Butte.

With practiced precision, the gang looted the town. Pack animals and wagons got loaded with food and supplies from the Mercantile, extra arms and ammunition from the gun shop, whiskey and women from the saloon. McDade and Swanson left the gunsmithy and broke into the marshal's office, next to the saloon.

Bart Blackwell's brother, Matthew, stared out from the single cell.

"Hey!" Matt started. "You boys come to bust me out?"

McDade looked at his partner. Swanson shrugged. They flipped a coin and Blackwell won. Tim slipped the big key into the lockcase in the cell door and Blackwell dashed out.

The two gunhands pulled the rifles and ammunition

from the marshal's wallrack, then headed out.

A spatter of rifle fire started up. The town's men had worked onto roofs and into good cover. They started making the main thoroughfare dangerous for the bandits.

Barlow cut the marshal down and dragged him behind his horse along the middle of the street to the end of town, turned and rode back to the saloon, defying the snipers, who had begun to multiply.

"Time to ride, Nathan," Jed suggested.

"We got horses for the whores?" Nathan queried.

"Right out of the livery," his brother replied.

"Load 'em out the back door, then head up to the hill where we left that idiot Blackwell," Nate directed, pointing at the saloon. "Then set this den of iniquity on fire. Burn it to the ground."

"Be a good way to keep the townsfolk busy, huh?" Jed opined.

Allison stood with the other doves, cringing against the wall on the first floor, near the back door. The madam heard some of the rustlers' talk and she realized they intended to take the ladies along with them.

"Let me slip back, Doris," Allison whispered to her number one girl, who stood next to her. "Cover me."

"Be careful," Doris admonished as her employer stepped back to the wall.

A small storage door, no bigger than a child, lay hidden behind the covey of young frontier entertainers, and Allison knew that Scruggs kept a sawed-off shotgun inside there for emergencies. She made sure the guard looked the other way, then bent down and opened the door.

Sure enough, the double-barreled scattergun sat at

the back of the storage closet. Allison hauled the weapon out and hoped the distraction she planned could get her girls free.

Allison did not know that the shotgun, though loaded, had not been checked or tended to for quite some time. Moisture and neglect settled in long ago. She pristinely stepped back to the front of her girls, smiled seductively at the single guard at the door, then raised the weapon belly high.

Slim Cranston's mouth formed a soundless "oh" and his eyes registered the pain he anticipated from the formidable gun that pointed at him. Before he could move, Allison pulled the trigger.

The primer snapped loudly and the damp powder fizzled like a photographer's mantle. Buckshot dribbled out the barrel with enough force to raise welts on Slim's skinny shins.

Allison realized instantly what had gone wrong. Without a moment's hesitation she threw down the defective Greener, turned and ran toward the stairs.

The girls began to scramble after her. A rifle butt in Doris' belly stopped that.

Still limping, Cranston coughed his way through the smoke and stepped clear of the tangle of fallen girls to see Allison dashing headlong up the steps. He fired randomly and caught the young madam in the inner side of her left thigh. Allison screamed and fell forward on the stairs. She quickly took note that the wound seemed light and kept her wits as she scrambled the rest of the way to the second floor. She had a derringer in her room and she intended to use it.

Cooper and several of his men emptied the stables of horses, running them off in all directions before putting a lucifer to the hay in the livery barn. The tinder-dry prairie grass caught with a whoosh and the marauders rushed to safety outside.

Jed Barlow dashed into the saloon at the sound of feminine squeals and gunfire.

"What the hell's going on?" he bellowed.

"One of the hookers tried to kill me," Slim Cranston answered. "I shot her, but she made it up the steps."

"Never mind that, Turkey Neck," Jed growled. "Get the rest of them out the back door. I'm setting a torch to this place."

From the stores in the saloon, the young Barlow dumped the strong smelling liquid on the floor and near the walls and bar. He smashed the partial bottles of liquor on the back bar that the gang couldn't haul off with them, then made a trail back to the rear door with more coal oil. He took a scrap of dress from one of the girls, soaked it in kerosene, then scratched a lucifer to life. In a moment, flames burst along the floor as the oil reached a burning temperature.

"But . . . Allison's in there," Doris wheezed out when the black smoke of the oil started turning to white as the wood caught.

"Is that the bitch what tried to kill me?" Cranston growled.

"She can get out the front door if she's a mind to," Jed Barlow told the girls.

Quickly Turkey Neck Slim and Jed tied the whores' hands together as they loaded them on horses. Cranston leered and stroked the inner thighs of his helpless charges as he hoisted them in place until Jed growled at him to stop.

In her room, Allison stopped the bleeding with a doily

she rested her toiletries on. She checked her derringer and hid behind her bed, waiting for the first bandit to come through her door. She'd locked it and hoped her girls had scattered.

She smelled something burning. Quickly Allison looked out the window.

Flames licked at the livery's walls. The madam gritted her teeth, then turned impatiently back to the door.

Nathan Barlow rounded up his men, all the time dragging Peters' body behind him. Matt Blackwell seized a horse and followed the bandits out of town.

They headed due south.

Eli rode due north, noting the volume of rifle fire continued to grow. He spotted smoke beginning to curl into the sky and prodded his horse harder.

Again, flames flickered around burning lodges and screams of Crow, Arikara, and Pawnee echoed in his mind.

Chapter Fifteen

Eli rode along the hard-packed trail toward Eagle Butte, watching the tendrils of white smoke turn into boiling black and gray towers whipped away by the north wind. Then he noticed a second cloud, this one low to the ground, brown and dusty, rising only sightly above the hills and thick tree cover.

It rolled in his direction.

The scout bounded from the saddle and led Sonny quickly to a wash with dense willow and cottonwood as cover. He put a hand over the animal's muzzle to stifle any outcry. Not a moment too soon.

Before he had a chance to pull his Winchester from its scabbard, thundering hoofbeats charged past his hiding spot and dust settled over him like a brown coat of snow. The Barlow gang disappeared over a rise with a speed that matched their arrival. Not before Eli had a chance to count their numbers and their booty, though.

He made it thirteen men. He recognized most of them as Barlow gang members from the raid he and the marshal had pulled on them so long ago. He also saw Matthew Blackwell, someone else Eli had counted on being hanged by now. Nine women slowed the outlaws slightly. Pack animals and wagons, loaded down with looted goods, ran behind the riders. Soon, they would take their toll as well.

Holten remounted and headed once again for Eagle Butte.

Ten minutes later he broke the ridge before the town and saw the place in chaos.

The Thunder Saloon and the livery stable burned out of control. Sparks flew in all directions and threatened every building in town. The people of Eagle Butte ran about aimlessly, disorganized and shaken by the ordeal. Some tried to fight the fire, a few attempted to round up horses, while still others stood dazed and studied the destruction, awe-struck.

Eli rode straight into the eye of the human storm. "Where's the marshal?" he shouted from his horse.

"They killed him," Luke wailed. "It was terrible. They shot him, then. . ."

"Don't dwell on it, man," the scout rebuked the smithy. "Organize a fire brigade and save the other buildings."

"But what about the wounded? They musta shot. . ."

"The women'll take care of the wounded. You fight the fire. Start with the saloon. It's closer to the other buildings."

Eli grabbed a wild-eyed little boy who dashed out onto the street from the boarding house. "Tommy!" Eli yelled to get the terrified ten-year-old to listen. "You wanna help?"

The lad's ears perked up and his eyes cleared. "Yes, sir."

"Get all your friends together and round up the horses. Can you do that?"

"Yes, sir, sure I can," he answered in a confident tone and took off with a purpose. Eli turned back to the blacksmith, who blushed over the clear-headed

182

reaction of the boy.

"Come on, Luke," Holten urged irritably. "A fire brigade!"

"Buckets!" Luke suddenly bellowed. "Opey, Jason! Run to my shop. I got a pile of buckets in the back room. Haul all the ones you can and get to the water trough out in front of the Thunder."

The blacksmith trumpeted orders to every man he saw, directing them into organization and, shortly, a line of men swamped water out of the trough and set to knocking down the fire with well-aimed bucketsful while others started climbing across the roofs of the adjoining structures, dousing out flames started by falling embers from the saloon fire. They smothered them with wet blankets and hacked away shingles with axes from the Mercantile.

In the boarding house, Mrs. O'Flannery and a grim Any Peters bandaged and administered to a half dozen wounded men and women. They had a collection of bullet holes, burns, and scrapes, with one broken arm from when the bank teller fell out a window trying to get a clear shot at the fleeing bandits.

"They killed Marshal Peters," the Easterner wailed and Amy bit her lip. "I'm telling you, we've got to get after them."

"Nobody's going anywhere," the wounded gunsmith whined. "I've had enough and if we try to be heroes, they'll just feel obliged to come back and do this to us again next year. Why, it all goes back to those damned army horses and the Injun cattle. It weren't our fight at all. Marshal Peters an' the scout here got us into this to begin with."

Eli felt a hot flush of red bite at his cheeks. Other

towns had suffered worse. Why was Eagle Butte coming on like whipped dogs?

"If you'd listened to Daddy, you would've been ready for them," Amy came scathing back. "He told you the Barlow gang was coming. You could have stopped them."

"We have to go after them," Eli added. "They have nine ladies with them."

"Whores," the gutless gunsmith scoffed. "They'll like it as well with the Barlows as here. You don't get yourselves killed over chippies."

Reverend Zeke walked briskly up the hill and in the cool, crisp air of the day felt better. If Eli made it to town, the marshal would have organized the men and shot the Barlow gang right to the Pearly Gates. Not through them, but close enough for Saint Peter to figure out the extradition arrangements. He'd been walking since he'd given the scout his horse, sleeping only a few hours next to a crystal clear stream with fish and animals of all description for company. He'd found himself feeling better for the exercise, not being jostled and dumped around by a horse. Maybe he'd go off next summer and walk acrosss the Black Hills. He could get Eli to introduce him around to all the Indians in those parts. Maybe he'd spread the Good News to the savages. . . .

A wisp of cooking smoke creeped out over the tree cover ahead and Zeke's happy wandering came to a close. He hefted his rifle in one hand, rearranged the blanket roll over his shoulder and started creeping forward, headed for high ground.

He edged up along a bluff that stuck high into the cold air before ending in a sheer cliff that dropped a good thirty feet before tapering more gradually to the flat out ahead. Zeke could see an encampment in the clearing at the base of the bluff. He recognized Nathan Barlow immediately. Worse, he saw some of his most staunch church goers, the soiled doves of the Thunder Saloon, being manhandled by the toughs.

The Barlow gang had hit Eagle Butte, the reverend reasoned, and had been so successful as to steal away the girls. He searched among their number but didn't see his good friend, Allison, in their midst. He offered a quick prayer that she had escaped.

Quickly a plan formed in the wiry young minister's mind. He knew exactly where the Barlow gang encamped. If he stole a horse he could get to town, round up the able-bodied men and strike the brigands before they escaped south. Barlow was so brazen, Smith thought, the religious hypocrite might take the same steamboat back to Kansas that he came on. The minister slipped down the hill and, favoring washes and storm-cut ravines, inched his way closer to the camp.

The loud voices of drinking men and grappling women met his ears as he began to crawl through deep buffalo grass that filled the clearing. He worked silently toward the single guard who stood, carbine in hand, leering at the ladies as they protested the attentions of the rustlers.

"What's wrong, sweetheart?" Cooper asked Doris. "You do this every day of your life. Why don't you undress and swallow my prod?"

Doris hung tenaciously to her clothes. "I beg your pardon, sir," the young dove answered coyly. "I am a lady

185

for hire. You have not offered me financial reward for my attentions." She kicked the gunman solidly in the shins. "And if ya did, I'd throw it in your face!" she screeched.

The laughter circled loudly around as Cooper hopped on one leg, a pained grin on his lips. "A real fighter," he hooted. "But she'll be great when I finally charm her out of her pantaloons."

"Why'd we stop so soon, Nate?" Jed asked off to one side.

"That den of evil doers ran like the children of Babylon at the foot of the tower," Nathan answered poetically. "We have wreaked our vengeance upon the miserable sinners and now we must rejoice and celebrate our righteous victory. Besides, I'm horny as hell," he added with a wink.

Mimi, a black-haired beauty with long legs and sweet full lips, got backhanded by Harry, who always liked it rough and urgent. He ripped at the girl's dress as Matthew and Bart Blackwell howled and cackled, teasing their peckers with rapid strokes as they watched the rustler slap the girl hard in the face again.

The guard, Jethro Poole, inched away from the horses toward the midday party, and Zeke Smith eased from behind the tree where he hid. The minister pulled a small knife from his pocket, carefully sliced the three lines that held the large number of horses in place and took one mount that still had its saddle on. Leaning low over the steed's neck, the preacher fired a shot across the other animals, then chased after them, screaming and howling like an Oglala raiding party. The animals scattered in every direction.

The loud report of Zeke's six-shooter jerked the bandits away from the ladies and toward their ready weapons. Cooper rolled over and whipped a Winchester into his hands. He fired a quick shot toward the fleeing horse thief. The other men scrambled after the scattering nags. All too late.

Zeke crested a rise, surrounded by the horses he'd released, and disappeared down the other side.

"That was that damned preacher man," John Hay cursed in awe.

"It can't be," Nathan countered. "God would not do that to me."

"Well, whoever it was is headed north and will prob'ly be in Eagle Butte in two, three hours."

The fires only smoldered now. No other building but the livery and saloon suffered any serious damage. The town set about caring for itself, as though hit by a storm or a tornado. A natural disaster, something that happened in the rough and woolly West, they could understand. So, in their minds, they tried to equate the Barlow raid with such events.

Eli helped with the gathering of arms. The Barlows had been thorough. They'd cleaned out the most likely places for weapons: the gunsmithy, the Mercantile, and the marshal's office, leaving the citizens of Eagle Butte low on ammunition and morale.

Tommy, the boy Eli had sent out looking for horses, came running breathless down the street. Puffs of dust rose from under his bare feet.

"Mister Holten! Mister Holten!" he cried. "They killed the old trapper, Mister Spurs."

Quickly several men, horseless, headed out for the high butte, where Old Man Spurs lived . . . and died.

"Why'd they kill an old man that didn't mean nobody any harm?" Luke asked.

"Probably because he recognized them and would have warned us about them," Eli explained. A thought crossed his mind. "Did old Spurs keep any spare rifles around?"

"Hell, yeah, the best. Down under his bed in a special box he made for them," Opey volunteered.

"Could you go up there and see if the Barlows found them?"

"Glad to." The bartender set out on foot after the men slready walking south.

Eli looked to the sun. It already leaned toward its daily death. He thought about Reverend Zeke. The minister traveled north, the Barlows ran to the south. Holten hoped the former infantryman would remember when to take cover.

Jason, the saloon owner, stumbled out of the rubble of his business, screaming. "'Help! Help me!" he yelled as he stumbled over the unburned wooden slats they had once called a sidewalk.

Eli trotted toward the barkeep and their eyes met. Jason's streaked and dirty face looked sick and he never took his eyes off the scout.

"It. . .it's Allison," he croaked. "She. . .she's back there."

Concern and anger crowded onto Eli's face. He pushed past the saloon keeper and ran into the burned and cumbling saloon.

A heap of partially burned clothes lay piled against the gutted staircase. Even before Eli reached the bundle's side he knew it was Allison.

Her hips shaped like a perfect heart when she bent from the waist to entertain and pleasure. Her petite and manicured fingers could barely wrap around Eli's wrist. Her feet and legs were rounded and her chubby, warm flanks couldn't be mistaken, even scorched and blackened. If there had been any doubt, her face hadn't been touched by flames.

"It must have been the smoke that done her," Jason volunteered from behind, a strangled sound in his throat. "If she could've lasted a dozen more steps she woulda made it to the back door."

A solid hard rock formed in Holten's chest and he scooped the light body into his hands. Carefully he carried her to the street, and for a moment he could understand the way the town felt. He'd lost more than he'd bargained for.

From the south a thundering horse came running wildly in, the black-suited form of the Reverend Smith holding on tenaciously to the reins of his lathered mount. "I seen 'em," he cried out. "I saw the whole lot of them. The Barlow Gang."

He leapt from the saddle and went running down the middle of the street. He came to an abrupt halt as Eli stepped out of the hotel, gently carrying his package of grief up the block. The minister raised his hands to his chest and a great sob escaped him. Then he silently fell in beside the scout. Grimly Eli set his face with coldblooded passion as Zeke melted into tears. Eli knew what he wanted, more than a cool beer or a good shot of whiskey. More even than a good time in bed, though with the same sort of soul-deep hunger. He wanted bloody revenge.

The gentle minister felt the moisture that slid down his cheeks in silent remembrance of the soiled dove he had loved and, though he did not know it, he suddenly shared Eli's desire for vengeance. He wanted to kill Nathan Barlow and all the men with him.

Amy Peters met them halfway to the boardinghouse. She had her father's extra revolver tucked into a sash across her riding dress. She grasped a Winchester in her left hand and a Spencer rifle in the other. "We're wasting time," she announced tersely. "Let's get going."

"Where do you figure to go?" Eli inquired.

The prim, handsome face of the beautiful woman pinched with hatred and anger. "You haven't stoved in, too, have you?" she accused. "The Barlow gang couldn't have gotten far. If we hurry we might be able to get to them before nightfall." Amy hefted the Spencer to her shoulder. "I'm going to kill me one Nathan Barlow and any of the others that want to get in my way."

"First of all," Eli choked out. "You're not going anywhere. You're a woman and you got no place in a posse. Second, we're not going this late toward evening. We'll get an early start in the morning, when we're all rested and we've got enough horses rounded up to mount sufficient riders to handle thirteen killers that are armed to take on a tribe of grizzlies."

"I'm going, Holten," she retorted bluntly. "I have to avenge my father and I don't figure there's a buck man enough in this town to do it for me."

The scout turned away from the furious young woman. He had no time to argue with foolishness. He had to make arrangements for a proper funeral for Allison, then he had to organize a posse.

190

The Barlow gang spent the rest of the day chasing down their mounts and, by the time dinner rolled around, not a man could muster the strength or inclination to struggle with the unwilling prostitutes, who huddled together in a corner of the camp, under the watchful gun of a serious guard. The sisters drew close together and pooled their warm bodies to keep the chill of the night from draining them.

"We still gonna keep the chips?" Art asked. "They ain't much use unless we can poke them."

"Tomorrow, about lunch time," Nathan answered. "You'll be so sweaty to stick your pecker in one of them, you won't know what to do with yourself. You'll have your pokey-pokey and to spare. Then we ride for Texas."

Chapter Sixteen

A temporary morgue had been set up in a tent against the side of the Mercantile. Eli tenderly carried Allison's body there. Many others had preceded him, wrapped in their private grief, though he took no notice of them. The face of the mortician looked like some mummified body in the desert, the yellow-brown skin hugging his bones. He looked mournfully up at the scout and directed him where to lay the corpse.

"Please accept my sincere condolences," he intoned in a professional manner. "Coffins are fifty dollars, seventy-five with lining."

Holten handed over the money in gold coin, which brought a slight, though pinched smile to the undertaker's face.

Zeke and Eli left the mortuary tent looking for a posse.

The menfolk huddled on the other side of the Mercantile from the temporary undertaking parlor, drinking whiskey the Barlows hadn't destroyed or stolen. They greeted the scout with sullen glances and uncertain mutters.

"I'm looking for a posse," Eli announced from the boardwalk. "You're going to have to supply your own ammunition and grub. We're gonna leave early tomorrow morning."

No one stirred.

"Come on," the scout urged. "Who's going?"

"I sure as hell ain't," the gunsmith spat. "I ain't getting killed for this stupid, shitty town. The danger's passed away. They got what they wanted and they're gone."

"But they have the ladies!" Reverend Smith bellowed.

None of the men responded. Demoralized, they stared into their bottles and pitied themselves. Several shuffled their feet like errant school boys.

"I ain't gonna risk my neck for a bunch of whores, Reverend," the gunsmith finally volunteered. "I'd think you'd be the last to worry about sinful scum like that."

" 'Sinful scum' you say?" Ezekiel warbled in the best voice of an evangelical minister. "Why, they're the worst kind of sinners. Aren't they, Brother Gunsmith? They roll around between the sweaty sheets, slapping their moist, hot bodies against some stranger who's got the price to buy their ass, and the Good Book condemns such goin's on, doesn't it?"

Zeke bent down low and his eyes pierced through the hearts of the men before him in the gathering gloom.

"But, Brother Gunsmith, you've sought refuge between those sheets every Saturday night since I came here. I think you prefer Lulu, the one with the tatoo, although sometimes you visit Mimi for variety."

The slender gunsmith's pock-marked face flushed scarlet. He opened his mouth to protest, then closed it again.

"If there's one thing I can't abide it's a hypocrite," Zeke continued. "The fact of the matter is, boys, that those gals offer a pleasant smile, a soft touch, and womanly bounty without which the town of Eagle Butte would be mighty grim. Think about the days ahead, men of the prairie. No frilly giggles from warm, cuddly creatures dashing genteely across the streets of our fair town, no sweet voices calling you by name and giving you a knowing wink and smile." The preacher pressed a hand to his chest in a dramatic gesture. "I don't judge. 'Judge not, lest ye be judged.' Why do *you* judge these ladies so callously? Now think of those filthy swine that killed our marshal and stole those angels of the Thunder Saloon from you, forcing their affections upon them, crushing Mimi's soft curves under their unwashed bodies, raping Doris and the others until the poor doves are raw and hurting. Do you want that to happen?"

"No!" the men cried out in chorus.

"Are you going to *let* that happen?"

"No!"

"I want to hear a halleluiah!"

"Halleluiah!" the gathered throng cried out.

Ezekiel led them in a chorus of *Onward Christian Soldiers*, then got them all deputized.

"A more soul-inspiring revival I have never attended," Eli dryly told Zeke.

"At least I was talking about something they were interested in," Zeke answered.

"You know, a power like that could be downright dangerous," the scout observed. The minister strolling at his side only grinned.

The Thunder Saloon had been Holten's shelter while in Eagle Butte, and all his worldly possessions had burned up with it, except for what had been stolen from him by the Barlows. All he owned now was his Remington and bowie knife, plus the clothes on his back and what he took from the dead bodies of the gunhawks at the prairie fire. With the livery stable gone the only other place for cover turned out to be Mrs. O'Flannery's boardinghouse.

"No swearing," the Irish widow commanded with steely eyes and gelatin jowls. "No guests in the room and *no drinking*."

Holten grimaced, reminded himself he'd be there for only a night, and took a room to the back of the hallway with a window looking out across the low hills that surrounded the town of Eagle Butte.

Eli kicked off his boots, loosened his clothing and hung his gunbelt on the bedpost. He lay on the bed and let his anger smolder.

Barlow and his cutthroats had killed the marshal. They'd killed his precious Allison. He still had to take care of Bart Blackwell, and now Matthew Blackwell joined the lengthening list of men Holten had to exact vengeance on.

The problem was there were so damn many of them. And then, they were good. Every last one of the Barlow gang was a deadeye shot. The scout felt his back and knew Bart Blackwell could shoot and figured his brother could, too. He might raise a posse of maybe twenty men. He suspected that wouldn't be enough. Barlow's peculiar talents worked well with a large number of men.

A knock came on the door.

Eli slipped the Remington from its holster that hung from the bedpost, rose and glided silently to the door. He stood to one side of the entrance and asked, "Who is it?"

"It's me, Mister Holten, Amy Peters."

"No guests in the rooms," Eli rumbled in a fair Irish brogue as he opened the door.

Amy Peters still wore her riding dress, a split twill skirt that allowed her to fork a regular saddle, a floppy hat that looked fashionable, although the scout knew how functional the wide brim could be on the unpredictable plains, and a tight leather blouse with fringes. Her eyes spoke of revenge as she silently stepped past Holten into the room, then stood there until he closed the door.

She turned and stared at him.

"Evening," he finally offered.

"Nathan Barlow murdered my father in his sickbed," Amy began. "I *must* go on the posse. I must have revenge."

"That's what started this whole thing," the scout noted. "The Barlows wanted revenge, now I want revenge and so do you. Tomorrow, the men and I'll ride and do them dirt and get the . . . ladies back."

"They killed little Allison," Amy charged. "Just for that I'd like to hang them."

"You . . . you knew Allison?" Eli asked. "No disrespect, but she was a . . . a. . ."

"Hooker," Amy finished, "I, uh, well . . . I knew her from church."

"Right."

"I'm going, Scout," the young woman announced and turned her sharp features to Holten. Eli felt stirrings in his loins. The first time he saw Amy he'd hoped she worked out of the Thunder Saloon. The late marshal's daughter had long, curly hair and soft, sparkling blue eyes, sensuous lips, and her clothing stretched and strained at the most appealing places.

"No," Holten finally answered. "You"re not going anywhere. It won't be safe out on this hunt."

"My father taught me to shoot, Mister Holten," Amy

countered. "Set me up on a hill with a Sharps and I'll plug the bastards at any distance you can name. I'm good with a Winchester and I can outride any man in this town."

"That, I doubt," Eli said flatly. "You're not going along."

The girl's hardened, angry features seemed to crumble with the scout's steadfast rejection.

"Look, Mister Holten," she started again in a softer voice, her expression sadder and more hurt than angry as she talked. "My father was everything to me. My maw died when I was seven and my dad's kept me by his side ever since. He could have left me with relatives back East, or for that matter turned me over to an orphanage, but he wanted me with him."

Her ravaged expression turned brittle and suddenly shattered with grief. She let a heart-rending sob break her lips, and tears spilled from her eyes.

"He's all I've ever had," she cried.

Eli wrapped an arm around the weeping woman. Her legs wobbled as her strength waned. Holten settled her on a corner of the bed. Amy buried her ruined face in the scout's chest and her salty tears stained his buckskin shirt.

"There, there," Eli comforted. "Everything's gonna be all right."

For a long time Holten rocked gently while Amy cried. Her pain seemed to be endless. She wept until every ounce of grief had passed, until a void filled her soul where the anger and tears had been.

Eli patted her back, alternating with a rubbing motion along her spine. Suddenly he straightened his own posture. Amy's hand, which had been wrapped around his waist, now delicately slid down between his legs.

Her eyes met his.

"Would you . . . would you mind if I stayed here for the night?" she inquired in a little-girl voice.

Eli stared deeply down into the windows of her soul. "You know, your father warned me not to get any ideas about you."

"Papa thought I was a virgin," Amy returned simply.

Their lips met, a long, hungry kiss that coiled their bodies around each other. They slid to the bedspread and began fumbling with each other's clothes.

Holten realized as he pulled Amy's blouse off over the top of her head that she wanted to be comforted, healed, and cared for, her grief and pain tearing wounds in her spirit that sought salving. Amy undid her skirt and squirmed out of it, leaving her in a waist-length shift and pantaloons. She reached behind her back and pulled a drawstring.

The lovely woman shrugged the thin cloth off her shoulders to expose creamy white orbs of firm, melon-sized breasts, with dark red nipples that hardened with Eli's gentle touch. As he took firm grasp on Amy's bounty, she pulled her pantaloons off and threw them over the side of the bed.

A slight shiver ran through her, the cold of the night chilling the room; or perhaps anticipation thrilled her.

Nimble fingers dug at Eli's clothing now as the scout slipped a work-hardened hand as gently as he could along the inside of Amy's thighs, then the dark thatch of curly hair between her legs.

Her mound felt fiery, its crevice already wet with welcome. Holten had to desist and raise his arms to let Amy pull his buckskin shirt off over his head. He lay back on the bed to the pillow as he wormed out of his trousers.

Amy, her thin waist and swelling hips undulating languidly as she moved, slid up next to the scout. She made a pretty pout as she glided a hand along his hairy chest, inspecting his many wounds and battle scars. The two fell silent for a long time, Eli slipping an arm under her shoulder. Amy pressed against the scout's side while her wandering hand sought out Eli's semi-hardened phallus.

"Allison said you were the best she'd ever had," Amy finally gusted out.

"Allison talked to you about an awful lot of personal things, if you don't mind my saying so," Eli remarked.

Amy turned her eyes back to his.

"She understood me," Amy explained. With that, the marshal's daughter kissed Eli's chest, his sternum, belly, abdomen, and finally, his swelling shaft. It responded to Amy's lips like Sonny did to sugar. It stretched toward them, all the time engorging with heated blood.

Solemnly Amy concentrated as her lips slipped over the dark red tip and Eli groaned. Would the preciously beautiful Amy find solace or peace, or just be able to forget her grief for a brief while here in his bed? Holten wondered on it as he sat up and kissed her back. Then he gently nudged and urged Amy around until, while she still labored with his shaft, he could inspect and titillate the petals and opening to her pulsing tunnel.

Entwined, they rocked and suckled at each other, administering to their diverse hopes and desires, willing each other to forget their hurt and loss.

Eli dug his tongue in between the pink folds of Amy's cavernous and inviting crevice, slathering along its open and inviting length. He worked and prodded in determined effort. Yet, every other moment, a picture of Allison in some daring outfit distracted the scout. He wound his hands under Amy's firm, tight rump and thought for a second about how the backside of the madam of the Thunder Saloon had been more rounded, though not quite as firm as Amy's.

Eli wondered if the lovely lady licking at his throbbing penis and gently kneading his tight sack of balls found herself distracted by thoughts of her father.

"To my knowledge," the one-eyed marshal had told him, "my daughter's a virgin, and that's a fantasy I care to feed."

Passion intruded now on Eli's morbid reflections. If Amy still grieved as badly as she had, she hid it well enough as she worked probing fingers along Eli's legs, buttocks, sides, and belly. She teased and slurped, nipped and swallowed the scout's excited love-spear. Holten used his fingers now on Amy's delectable pink dessert that flowed richly with anticipation. He found the tiny, throbbing device at the top of her cleft and began to manipulate it like a small penis. Amy shuddered with delight. He tasted her woman's liquor and savored the passion that secreted from her flower. He couldn't wait much longer. His desperate hunger now blocked out anything else. He extracted his hard shaft from Amy's protesting throat, swung around and poised himself over the willing, full form of the marshal's daughter.

Amy's legs spread, then wrapped around his waist.

"Pleasure me, Eli," she whispered. "Comfort me."

The hungry tip of Holten's stretched war-horse inched closer to the dark and foaming portal to Amy's soul. It touched the leafy fronds that blossomed around the dark red orifice, and Amy gurgled her approval, undulating her hips invitingly.

Holten slipped the head of his adverturous spear into the tight entrance, squeaking by, buttered with her love lotion, then worked it to the side, twisting and teasing with building speed.

"Deeper, Eli," she begged.

He did not succumb to her wishes at once, only intensified her desperate insistence until finally delilvered, a plunging drive into the deep waters of her limpid pool.

Amy exploded from within and squelched screams of a dynamite climax. Holten's very full presence was enough to wrack her with orgasms. The scout, though, had only started.

The woman's dream-filled eyes lazily studied his as he began to slowly gyrate his hips, and the probing lance twisted and slid against the all-encompassing walls that clung tightly to it.

Amy worked her own hips with deliberate care, thrilling to the driving mass that filled her like none other had ever done. A pretty smile, like that of a child, graced her lips as they built momentum and speed into their lovemaking.

Suddenly Amy ran ahead. Her hips went wild and her breath became tortured gasps and hungry pleadings as she once again exploded over the peak of desire and shuddered with the completeness of her fulfillment.

"Now . . . now . . . now . . . NOW! she panted in time with the hot waves of climax that burst over her like fiery surf.

Eli couldn't stop now. He charged on into the creamy depths, stroking and swaying, attacking and retreating so quickly the motion merged into a blur. Amy joined him and together they ran headlong toward the cliff and the abyss that lay beyond it.

Unhesitatingly, they leaped into the unknown and landed in a blazing river that burned and seared as Eli delivered his life force with uncontrolled excitement.

The couple fell into a heap, the long, lanky body of the scout draped over the comely figure of the girl. They waited for their breath to come to a vague semblance of normal. Eli twisted and maneuvered them under the covers.

"We'd best get some sleep," Holten suggested.

"Let me go with the posse, please," Amy begged. "I promise I won't be in the way."

"You can't come, Amy . . . uh. . ." He paused, hesitant and surprised at the words he wanted to say. At last Eli succumbed. "That is, if you come, please be careful. I. . .wouldn't want to lose you now."

As it turned out, Amy spent most of the night waking the scout with hungry teasings of his manhood, urging him time and again to passionate wrestling matches. Apparently, Eli thought, Amy's grief was only outdone by her lust.

"You're not natural," Holten told the beautiful apparition that danced above him on his shaft.

"I was born this way," Amy grunted, an animal smile stretching her lips as she kneaded her breats and bounced and rocked on his rigid staff. "I can't remember a time in my life I didn't hunger for men. What most girls cherish until their wedding day I wanted to lose by the age of four. I got rid of it two years later, too, to a very surprised boy of ten." She bent down and let her swaying melons jiggle above Eli's enraptured eyes. "I've had to be awful careful, luring kids to the haymow at first, later sleeping with strangers who didn't know who

202

I was, jumping farm boys as they headed out of town. It woulda broke Papa's heart to know what a slut his daughter was."

"And Allison helped," Holten added with a grunt. "She set up the rendezvous with all those strangers?"

Amy nodded between gasps.

"Yes," she cried as her moment of glory rushed on her. "That's why I knew so much about you. Allison was a real friend. Oh, Lord! Here I come again!"

The closet harlot danced madly above the scout, until her desperate passion grew sated . . . for the moment.

Morning came much too soon.

Chapter Seventeen

Nate Barlow stared at the rising sun and cursed Reverend Smith one more time. They had only found half of their horses the night before and they would need an awful lot more before the gang could move on. After that, though, what then?

Nate thought of the open plains of Texas and the cattle being herded to their winter forage, of the easy pickings there. Not for rustling of course, with having to keep and care for them for so long before getting the ornery critters to market. Merely for eating, stealing a prime head or two from time to time to live off the fat of the land.

" 'See the lillies of the field,' " Barlow spoke aloud. " 'They toil not, neither do they sew.' " That's how God meant for Nathan Barlow to be, he thought, living off the largess of the land and witnessing for Him.

First things first, though.

Nathan walked over to the huddled pile of soiled doves and kicked at the prettiest one, Doris.

"Wha . . . !" She started and looked around crusty-eyed.

"Pull your skirt up," Nathan ordered. "I'm hungry."

"I ain't gonna have nothing to do with you," Doris countered rebelliously.

"Look," Nathan pressed, one hand massaging his

swollen organ through the heavy cloth of his trousers. "This ain't fun and games no more. I'm achin'. You're a chippie, relieve me."

"No," Doris spat.

"What're ya gonna do with us?" Mimi asked, coming awake with fear in her eyes.

Nathan looked away.

"Hadn't thought on that," he admitted. "I know! We'll sell you to the Indians for horses."

A startled gasp ran through the waking girls.

"Maybe take you south of the border and sell you to banditos. Or one of them fancy Mezkin sportin' houses."

One girl cried out in anguish.

"You'll never get away with it," Doris declared. "The men of Eagle Butte will come for you and kill you all."

"No," Nathan replied conversationally. "They're too busy fightin' fires. Besides, they got no one to lead them, with the marshal dead. I've a mind to go back there, though, and hang that Ezekiel Smith."

"You leave Reverend Zeke alone!" Wanda, a beefy Nordic girl, demanded.

"Reverend my ass!" Nathan snarled at her. "How many ministers do you know who steal horses? Yeah! A horse thief! That's a hangin' offense."

A cunning look came to the rustler's eyes. "I tell you what, girls," Nate started. "I'll make a deal with you. I got twelve horny men and two horny Blackwells. Now, if you really worked them loose, I mean leave them feelin' all relaxed and satisfied, walkin' all wobbly kneed, I'd be tempted to let you go. Right here to yerselves. And we'd mosey on without you. Sound like a fair shake?"

Doris looked back at her charges. She was the number one lady and had taken over when Allison escaped. The

205

girls looked to her for leadership. Doris turned back to Barlow.

"We're gonna have to talk about it," she told him.

"Fine. You do that. The boys are gonna go huntin' for more horses and when they get back . . . I expect an answer. Remember this. . ." His eyes narrowed with menace. "One way or another . . . we're sure as God gonna fuck you."

Eli and Amy arrived at the Mercantile before the sun broke the horizon. Already the preacher had the horses saddled and the men fed. The two late-comers got bacon, eggs, and pancakes served up in a tall stack on their plates.

"Eat, eat," Zeke pressed. "Time's a wasting."

Washing the heavy meal down with coffee, Amy and Eli quickly joined the rest of the posse and they headed out of town, due south.

Altogether they numbered eighteen men and Amy. Eli tried to figure their odds.

"They couldn't have left that spot where I stole . . . er, got the horse," Smith told Eli. "I ran their remuda every way I could. It must have taken those varmints the rest of the day to find them all, and they'd have to camp there for the night."

"Why'd they stop so soon after leaving town?" Eli wondered aloud.

"To *harass* the women." The minister pointed a finger heavenward. "I hope I interrupted *that*, too."

Quickly a plan formed. The posse would swing around and come to the large clearing from the west. A gully ran under the bluff and that would let them cut the

Barlow gang off. Clearing couldn't be more than two hour's ride away.

The search for the horses took a damn sight longer than McDade, Swanson, and Hawkins had expected. A large number of the animals had run west, and the three men went after them. They pressed the critters as they rode full out. When they came to a stream, Hawkins leaned over and studied the tracks. The fleeing hoof-prints turned north and the riders followed.

"This tree cover is so damned thick," McDade noted with awe. "A feller could build a whole town full of houses with this much wood."

"We can follow the tracks," Swanson planned aloud. "But maybe, if we could get to a rise, or the top of one of these trees, we could see those animals of ours."

"They'd favor the clearings and the water, wouldn't they?" McDade asked.

"So far they have," Hawkins observed.

The men rode to a slight rise and then Hawkins, the smallest of the trio, scampered up a tall lodge-pole pine until he broke free of the ground cover to look on tree-tops and rolling hills for as far as he could see. He pulled the field glasses McDade had given him out of his jacket pocket and looked for clearings among the pine thickets.

A thin break in the foliage snaked north to south toward them, and Art spotted horses in it, headed their direction. His pleased expression altered suddenly when he realized these weren't the critters they had come looking for. He moved quickly and quietly down the tree.

"Posse," he hissed at his compatriots.

"How many?" Leroy inquired.

"Too many," Hawkins told him.

Back at the camp, though few of the men had come in yet, Nathan felt the pressure build with every carefully deliberate stroke he laid into Doris. His reddened shaft glistened with her moisture and his impending eruption built tension that seemed to pierce his heart. The force grew until at last he exploded and groaned with satisfaction. Nate used short stabs of his fleshly weapon to work the last drop of his life force into the receptacle that rested on all fours in front of him.

"Damn good, young lady," the pleasured gang leader wheezed. "Now, that wasn't so bad, was it?"

"I hardly felt a thing," Doris responded. Her insult was wasted on Nathan, who considered himself a divine lover.

Nathan pulled out with a growing smile on his lips, then hitched up his pants and stood. Bart and Matt Blackwell had grown hungry and returned early, looking for food. They witnessed Nate's final moments of passion and knew a different sort of famine.

"Can we wrastle 'em now, Mister Barlow?" Bart asked, eyes glowing.

"Not until the others get back," Nate responded.

"But . . . you got laid."

The look Nate gave Bart would have torn the hanger on a new asshole.

" 'Course we can always wait," the Blackwell brother hastened to say.

Nathan looked around the open ground. "Where is everybody?" he demanded.

"They'll be along," Jed soothed. He walked to his brother's side as Nate headed for the hot coffee.

"It's gonna be a shame to leave the ladies behind," the

208

younger Barlow commented.

"We ain't leavin' anything," the leader asserted. "They're righteously earned booty and we'll sell them to the highest bidder."

"You told them you were gonna let them go," Jed countered.

"I lied," the older Barlow admitted. He continued with a defensive expression on his face. "It's all right to lie to chippies. They're sinners, after all, doomed to the Flame."

"Just checking," Jed said through a smile. He turned his attentions to Mimi.

Three riders broke into the open from the west, riding hard toward the camp.

"There's a posse comin', Nathan," Hawkins cried from the back of his horse before even stopping.

"How many?"

"I counted eighteen," Art answered. "The Reverend's with them."

"Why, of course he is," Nate chortled. "The little thief couldn't help himself but to come back to the scene of his crime."

Hawkins studied his boss' face before continuing. "Someone else is with them," he added hesitantly. "The scout. Eli Holten."

Barlow stared at his man for a long time, this new piece of revelation slowly sinking in.

"He must have killed Bill and Tunney," McDade added.

"And the Reverend must have kilt ol' Abe," Swanson chimed in. Barlow didn't answer. He walked a little past the camp, clasped his hands together and looked heavenward.

"'My God, my God,'" he intoned in a prophet's mournful voice. "'Why have You forsaken me?'"

"Gee, Mister Barlow," Matthew Blackwell said. "That was purty."

Nathan turned to look at the two brainless brothers. "You Blackwells," he ordered. "You take the harlots. Go east somewhere."

"We could set up an ambush with them," Jed suggested. "Leave them here, get the posse's attention."

Nathan studied the grimly smiling faces of the soiled doves as he thought, then shook his head.

"No," he finally said. "They'd start screamin' and tryin' to save their precious preacher. Might warn them off. Best to get them out of here."

"All right, you whores," Bart growled, savoring the feel of power. "Let's get your asses out of here."

"Just walk them into the trees," Jed ordered deflatingly.

"Yes, sir, Mister Barlow," Matthew muttered back.

"Those boys are so dumb they might shoot us 'cause we were in range," Swanson sighed, watching the herd of poontang wandering eastward.

"Best to have them with the other trash," Nate said. "If we have any extra horses, they can hold on to those, too."

Doris whispered something to Annie, a girl of seventeen, whose expertise lay in her little-girl act that brought no end of pleasure to her special customers. A plot got hatched in the covey of working girl quail.

The outlaws in the camp rode out and quickly rounded up all the other gang members. Some had gathered most of the horses, and the extra mounts were left in the care of the Blackwells.

"If they were smart," Barlow started to say, as

Hawkins, with Swanson and McDade helping, drew a map in the dirt, "they'd come up this gully and cut us off from the rear. And with Holten with them, that's what they're gonna do. So we'll ride out, get good and hid along the top of that gulch and have ourselves a turkey shoot."

From a short distance away, Cranston shot him a dirty look at what he believed to be mention of his hated nickname.

"Holten will probably come down first to scout the camp," Cooper pointed out.

"We'll hit them long before they get anywhere near our camp," Nathan assured the gunman.

Bart and Matt sat against a tree, guns lazily covering the soiled doves. Their faces wore bored expressions. Doris smiled at Annie and nodded. Annie grinned back and prepared herself.

"Oh!" she cried out in mock surprise, looking at the trees.

"Keep the noise down," Matthew barked.

"What's wrong, dear?" Doris inquired solicitously.

"I . . . I'm so . . . embarrassed," Annie wailed.

"What's the ruckus?" Bart demanded irritably, stepping toward the crowd of girls.

"I. . . I'm . . ." Annie drew it out. "I'm having withdrawal pains."

"Oh, poor dear," Lulu cooed sympathetically.

"I'm ever *so* embarrassed," Annie repeated, covering her face as she spread her legs slightly.

"Withdrawal? Bullshit!" Bart spat. "What the hell is she talking about?"

"Have ya ever seen a lush who needs a drink and doesn't get it?" Doris asked, impatience in her voice.

211

"She's a drunk?" Matt queried.

"No," Lulu informed the brothers, as though the obvious stood in front of them and they refused to see.

"Think about it, boys," Mimi started. "A girl has a man, any man, lots of men, every day, as many as ten, twelve times a day."

The Blackwells stared bug-eyed.

"I just love to frolic," Annie whined, running her tongue across her lips as a hand fell to her crotch.

"Then," Mimi continued the fabricated tale, "all of a sudden, no sex. None for a whole day."

"And a whole *night!*" Annie added with a soulful groan. "I'm in pain."

"It comes on so sudden," Doris confided to Matthew.

"Here, sweetheart," Lulu offered, pulling Annie's dress up. "Let me see if I can help."

Lulu, the one with the popular tatoo, fell between Annie's legs and set to licking the pretty girl's moist, pink fronds.

"Oh, that does feel good," Annie announced, fumbling with her small, pert breasts. With some assistance, she wriggled out of her clothes, then stretched and undulated on the ground. She worked her nipples to hard, brown knobs on her white, soft breasts, which she kneaded and squeezed, and then she turned to Matthew and blew him a kiss.

"Damn!" the Blackwell boy cursed, a large bulge rapidly growing behind the buttons of his fly. "Lookit that!"

"I still say it's bullshit," Bart growled.

"Is bullshit what's makin' yer pecker stiff?" his brother teased.

Both lads quickly opened their trousers and set to playing with themselves, putting aside their rifles to ma-

212

nipulate their throbbing rods.

"Oh, no!" Mimi cried as she spread her legs. "I'm going into withdrawal, too."

Another round of cooing concern rippled through the girls. Doris clucked at her sister in service and bent down between Mimi's legs to administer Lulu's cure for the pretended ailment.

"It's not helping anymore!" Annie shrieked. "I need a man!"

"I'm a man," Matthew cried out.

"You are?" Annie asked, her dumbest look on her face.

"Hell, yeah" Matt panted hysterically as he flogged his short, reddened penis. "So's my brother."

"Two girls in heat . . . two men," Doris noted happily. "Now, why didn't I think of that?"

"Would you help me, Mister Blackwell, please?" Annie asked Matt in her little-girl voice as she turned on her act. "I've just turned thirteen and I ache so for a big, long thing like yours." Lulu pulled away from the girl and idly began to massage her own tingling mound.

"Hell, sure," Matt agreed eagerly, slipping his suspenders and pulling down his trousers.

"Hold it!" Doris protested. "What about Mister Barlow? What would he say?"

"Who cares?" Bart shrieked as he dropped his drawers. They gathered around his knees and he waddled quickly to Mimi, who spread her legs extra wide and beckoned him down.

Matthew knelt first, then, on his knees, crawled to Annie's dripping orifice. With one quick lunge he dug into the girl's spicy-scented furrow.

Doris smiled, kissed Bart on the ear, then rose as the

other girls swarmed around, giggling, to join into the fracas, each one now claiming to be in withdrawal.

All except Lulu and the number one lady. They walked over to where the Blackwell boys had left their rifles.

First the two girls emptied the chambers of the weapons, to make sure they didn't go off accidentally and bring anyone around, then they returned to the writhing mass of bare legs and buttocks and the unsuspecting Blackwells.

Lulu grabbed her rifle by the barrel, aimed the butt at the base of Matt's skull and brought it way back. Then she slammed it to her mark as hard as she could.

The junior-grade desperado arched his back, rigid as a lodge-pole pine, and ejaculated prematurely as his surging phallus went limp. Then he fell unconscious on top of Annie.

Doris lined her rifle barrel to the top of her victim's head, while he gleefully bored into Mimi, totally unaware of what happened to his brother. The petite young dove drew the rifle high over her head while the other girls appreciatively watched, then brought it down with a skull-breaking crunch.

Mimi watched Bart's eyes cross. A giddy smile graced his face. The girl slid to one side and the Blackwell boy hit the thick bed of pine needles.

"There, now," Doris announced as she slapped her hands together as though to knock the dust loose. "A good day's work, girls. The next step is to warn the posse. Who wants to have fun riding a horse bareback?"

Chapter Eighteen

Eli and Zeke led the group in a circle around to the west. They followed a stream that cut a clearing through the thick forest that extended all the way to the Black Hills. The eighteen men in the posse skirted around where Zeke had said the Barlow gang camped out. Then headed for a gulch the minister had used to sneak up on the encampment.

Suddenly, from the thickest part of the stand of pine, two horses trotted out. Bouncing on the animals' bare backs came Doris and Mimi, holding on tenaciously to the mounts' manes.

"Reverend Zeke!" Doris cried out in between bounces. "Reverend Zeke. They know you're coming."

The menfolk crowded around the jiggled ladies, questions and comments piling over each other.

"That didn't feel half bad," Mimi noted, stroking the knobby spine of the nag she rode.

"Where are the other girls?" Zeke demanded.

"We all escaped," Doris said through a giggle. "The rest took off for Eagle Butte. We came to warn you."

"In fact, that was a lot of fun," Mimi added, petting the horse's throat.

"Where are they waiting?" Eli inquired, his mind working on alternative plans.

"They've got the gulch covered. We heard them say

they were going to ambush you there."

"Boys," Eli remarked to the other men "We got them."

"Why should we bother now?" the gunsmith interrupted. "The girls are safe."

"They got your guns, your ammo, your winter supplies, not to mention they emptied your bank," Eli reminded the reluctant posse man. "Besides, we can wipe them out to the man from this position."

"Let's slaughter them," Reverend Smith growled.

Eli scouted forward, Zeke close behind. The scout climbed a tall hill a mile from the ravine, then crawled up a tree that gave him an unrestricted view of the clearing and the gulch.

Holten could see the gang had found the girls were missing. Nate and Jed scrambled madly around while others broke camp. Sentries had spread out to forewarn of any approaching posse. He also noted something across the bluff. Eli studied the high ground on the north side of the gulch.

Although better hidden than could be detected by most whitemen, Holten marked the location of a number of Sioux warriors, watching the low ground like wolves sizing up a flock of sheep. The scout felt sure that Big Wolf had come and with many friends.

A sparkling idea occurred to Eli. So clean and pure, it could have flowed from melting snow. The scout shinnied down the tree and gave the preacher a big smile.

"You go tell the boys to make camp, settle down and get comfortable. Did you hear anyone say where that circuit judge went?"

"Lantry," Zeke replied. "I could get him here right quick."

"Then ride, Zeke," the scout answered. "We're gonna

do this like Orsen Peters would have wanted it."

Cooper touched his aching balls as he cinched his saddle down. "I purely missed my chance on those pussy-peddlers," he said, bemoaning his loss.

"We could go after them," Nate offered. "But they're for certain gonna warn that posse and then we'd be wiped out, right here or at that ambush pass. We got no choice. We gotta get while there's still time."

"Mister Barlow," Matt Blackwell whined from where he lay, strapped tightly to a pine tree. "We're sorry. Truly we are."

"I forgive you, boy. Both of you." Nate stepped toward the two men, tied head to toe around the base of a thick trunk.

"You gonna let us go?" Bart asked anxiously.

"No," the rustler leader replied. "I forgave you. I didn't say I'd clasp you to my bosom and forget your transgressions."

"What are you going to do with us?" Matt pressed, fear making his voice quaver.

"Leave you." Barlow glanced around the clearing at the preparations for the gang's flight. "You see, a town like Eagle Butte needs to take revenge. I understand that, although it's powerful un-Christian of them. If they can take you back and hang the both of you, they'll be less likely to come after us."

"That's mightly smart figurin', Mister Barlow," Bart complimented.

"Fear God, boys," Nate solemnly advised them. Then he turned and mounted his horse. "Fellers, let's get the hell out of here."

Eli crossed the ravine far enough down so that the Barlow sentries would not see him and Sonny, then headed for the high ground. He knew long before he reached the bluff that a dozen pairs of eyes watched him. He rode tall and proud until Big Wolf stepped from the cover close to the flat top of the bluff.

"It is good to see you *on* your horse, Tall Bear," Big Wolf greeted with a twinkle of mischief in his eyes.

"It is good to see you here, my friend," Eli answered in Lakota.

"I shamed the council for their cowardice after you left," the war chief informed him. "I went and found the Cheyenne who had lost their sons. We have twelve Dakota and five Cheyenne braves here, ready to make war on the bad whitemen."

"I have many men with me as well," Eli told him. "We could kill the evil men that we seek, but I think Barlow would escape, and I want him and his brother most of all. Will you help me with a plan I have?"

"Let us hear your plan," Big Wolf answered. "So long as it does not include losing more ponies." The broad-shouldered warrior seamed his face with a teasing smile.

"First," Holten continued, ignoring the jibe, "did you bring some women to take care of your camp?"

The Barlows moved quickly toward the Cheyenne River, plotting a course back for the Missouri. They had more money and supplies than they could have imagined. Eagle Butte turned out to be a right rich little town. The one thing they lacked, however, was what they'd once held and the Blackwells had let slip away.

"All that purty poontang," McDade whined. "All that fluff an' we spent the whole damn night sleeping!"

"Whatever you do, boys," Slim Cranston told his partners, "don't bend over. I'm so horny none of you are safe."

"Go to hell, Turkey Neck," Big Jack Glenn snapped at him.

"I'll tell you right now, Nate," Jed confided to his brother. "I've never seen our people so riled."

"If we hadn't brung 'em with us, we wouldn't miss 'em so bad," Nathan observed. "I sure wish I could do something to help."

A rider charged quickly from the north, a trail of dust kicking up behind him.

"See anything?" Cooper asked his man, Jake Day.

"I stayed until they rode into the clearing, Coop," Jake answered. "They must've been warned 'cause they didn't come out of the gully."

"What'd they do with the Blackwells?" Nathan inquired.

"Two fellers hauled them off in the direction of Eagle Butte."

Nathan nodded thoughtfully. "They'll hang before the sun sets tomorrow. An' may God have mercy on their souls."

"Anyone following us now?" Jed interrupted.

Day shrugged.

"They might in time," he replied. "A couple of them looked at our tracks, but they don't have any extra horses and they seemed a little confused as to what to do.

Couldn't quite make up their minds to follow."

"You see Holten or that preacher-man?" Nathan queried.

"I didn't see Smith," Greenwood hedged, "and I don't know what Holten looks like."

"We got them beat, then," Nathan predicted. "The Children of the Tower of Babylon. They'll spend the rest of the day arguing whether to come after us. Then they'll get liquored up tonight in camp and ride home tomorrow."

The gang strung out and continued their southward march.

"I want to beat my meat, that's what I want," Shank O'Niel grumbled.

"We've been riding all day," John Hay spat. "No noon meal break and no chippies. When do we get something out of all this?"

"The boys are gettin' downright mutinous," Jed warned when he trotted up beside his brother, who had taken the lead.

"There just ain't anything I can do out here about their woman hunger."

Another outrider, a gunhand called Jackson, came at a gallop, this time from the south.

"The banks of the Cheyenne is just over this rise, Mister Barlow," Jackson announced. "There's a good ford to cross a half mile down stream. I saw some cookin' smoke from that ways, though."

Immediately Nathan straightened up and took notice. "See anyone out there?"

"No, sir. Least ways, no whitemen," the rider replied. "I can mosey back and take a closer look. The camp that smoke is comin' from must be a good mile and a half further downstream."

"Take Art with you. He's got sharp eyes and knows the local Injuns if it's them." Nathan looked back over his horse. "The rest of you break for a couple of hours. Set up sentries and get some grub goin'."

Art Hawkins and the gunslick called Jackson rode until they hit the Cheyenne River, an untamed roll of red-brown water that cut down out of the Black Hills, then ended, feeding into the Missouri. The two men turned east and followed the bank until they spotted several tendrils of smoke rising into the sky before being whipped away by the north wind.

The Cheyenne took a sharp turn over rolling rapids, cutting north to slip around an imposing bluff, before returning to its southeasterly ambling.

The two desperadoes gained high ground on the northern side of the river. Hawkins pulled a borrowed pair of field glasses from his saddlebags and reconnoitered the camp across the stream.

Tipi lodges formed a circle on the southern bank of the Cheyenne. Fires in the center of the makeshift village put the smell of cooking meat in the air. Jackson sniffed at the aroma, imagining the savor of well-cooked buffalo.

"What do you make of it?" the gunhawk asked.

"Sioux by the looks of them," Hawkins replied. "Must be a hunting party. There's no children in camp and only a few women. Sort of late in the year for them to be this far north, though."

"Savages," Jackson scoffed. "I don't think anyone can predict what they'll do next."

"There's only two, maybe three braves in the whole camp. The others must be out on the hunt."

"That's bad. We don' know where they are."

"Least we know where they aren't," Hawkins countered, staring long and carefully through the glasses.

Neither man could have seen the small mirror further downstream flash sunlight toward the Sioux camp. Thunder Woman, observing the gleaming reflection, nonchalantly stopped what she was doing and walked quickly to the water's edge. There she stripped her buckskin clothing off and sat down on a flat rock next to the river. She splashed her feet in the eddied swirls, then began to lower herself into the rushing cold stream.

"Lookit that!" Hawkins hooted in a whisper.

"What?"

"That squaw just stripped and she's playin' in the water."

"That must be pretty cold," Jackson said.

"Hell, who cares?" Hawkins gulped. "I tell you she looks like she could warm the whole damn Cheyenne with a body like that. A little chubby, but I'd let her set my wick on fire."

"Let me see," Jackson prodded as he reached, then wrestled for the field glasses.

Thunder Woman spent a lot of time washing her breasts and upper torso, teasing and kneading her nipples, before stepping out of the river to begin to dry off. She did her best to look normal, although the water had chilled her body nearly to her stoic limit.

"Shit!" Jackson exploded. "And there's only a couple or three menfolk around."

"We gotta get back to Barlow," Hawkins puffed. "Reminds me of a soddy we once hit."

The Barlow gang could barely contain itself.

"Squaws," John Hay echoed. "I owned a squaw in Kansas for a year or two. She laid you like a plow horse. Worked like a mule."

"How many?" Harry Lemley asked, licking his lips.

"I counted three," Hawkins replied. "And there's three older braves. It's definitely a hunting party."

"Or a raiding band," Nathan offered.

"Hey! Wouldn't that be something?" Shank O'Niel guffawed. "We raid them while they're out raiding some poor homestead?"

"No one said we're hittin' this camp yet," Jed coolly growled at the horny men.

Silence came over the eleven hardcases.

"Those squaws are slippery. They run like mad," Nathan started. "If we hit a camp like that, there's a good chance they'd get away."

"We go in from two sides," Hawkins suggested. "Like we did at Eagle Butte. Hell, if we can take out a whole whiteman's town, we can knock over three old Injuns and the camp squaws."

Nathan looked out across the encampment. The men stayed silent while they waited breathlessly for his decision. Finally he nodded.

"A man's gotta do what a man's gotta do," he declared.

The Barlow gang crossed the Cheyenne upstream of the Indian village and made a cold camp, knowing how well the Sioux could spot signs of strangers in their area. Anticipation stretched at the bandits' trousers as they waited for morning.

Nathan sent out scouts at down to study the Indian position further. They reported back an hour later. The camp still looked empty and there was no sign of the Indian hunting party. No warriors except for the old men. A thick stand of trees grew north of the camp. The bluff blocked sight to the west, though riders could pass under it on the river bank. There lay little cover east along the course of the Cheyenne.

Cooper and his men, Greenwood, McDade, Swanson, Shank O'Niel, Big Jack Glenn, and Slim Cranston, snuck wide to the north, around the bluff's back side, to come in above the camp. Nathan and his boys, Jed, Hawkins, Hay, and Chub Kennedy, and two gunhands, Welles and Day, came in under the bluff on the bank of the river.

From the moment Barlow could see the camp, the Indians spotted him and stirred into action, stepping forward to challenge the approaching whites, casually scooping rifles into their hands.

Barlow let his men close within easy shooting range, then pulled his Winchester and fired at the closest old brave.

"Get 'em, boys!" he yelled.

The warrior's shoulder grew a red flower that blossomed with a spurt of blood. The brave spun and yelled his indignation as he collapsed from the impact. That's when things finally went wrong for the Barlow gang. If He ever had, God no longer rode with Nathan Barlow.

Cooper wheeled his horses through the stand of trees as his men spread out. When Barlow's shot signaled them, they started anxiously to push through the pine, looking to gather up any squaws that tried to escape to the north or east.

A moment later, the rider felt something fall hard on his horse. A war club snapped across his right ear. He bounced off his mount, with a contorted-faced Cheyenne hanging onto him.

Then it rained vengeful Cheyenne and Sioux on all of Cooper's men. Six warriors fell like huge hail stones from their hiding places they had occupied since before daylight. In their haste, Barlow's scouts hadn't looked for hidden men or horses. The young Cheyenne braves took Cooper and three of his men prisoners without firing a shot. Only Glenn, Shank O'Niel, and Cranston escaped. The latter wore a feathered shaft in one thigh. Regardless, they didn't stop to join the others in battle.

Unaware of this turn, Barlow and his boys charged screaming into the circle of lodges, and suddenly the closed flaps to the tipis burst open. Five Sioux and ten townsfolk stuck their rifles out and aimed at the horses, determined to trim the mounts out from under the seven men.

Nathan Barlow, suddenly confused and out-generaled, wheeled back toward the west. He expected his mount to whinny and collapse at any second or feel the bite of a bullet rip at his own flesh from the fusillade of slugs. The anticipated fate didn't come.

He kicked at his horse, urging it to more speed, ranging along the bank, returning to where he had ridden across.

Amy Peters took Old Man Spur's favorite buffalo rifle and carefully adjusted the rear sight. Only then did she remember to shoot the horse, if possible. She cocked the weapon and squeezed on the trigger.

The sound of thunder echoed all the way to the Black Hills. Barlow willed his animal to fly for safety in the camp they'd set up. Fresh horses waited there for a mad dash to the Missouri and North Platte, Nebraska.

Suddenly the top of Nathan's horse's head popped inward. Blood and watery, gray brain matter flew in all directions. Some splashed on Barlow's face and shirt. Then he catapulted wildly over the animal's ears.

Behind him, Eli watched the roan go down to Amy's crack shot and grabbed up the braided leather reins of a pony tied to a nearby lodge. He charged up the hill after the escaping gang leader.

Chapter Nineteen

Nathan Barlow, on foot, ran for the cover of the bluffs. He pulled his converted Remington. His Winchester had been lost in the fall from his horse. The scout saw the rustler grab his weapon and drew his .44. He eared back its hammer, then urged the Sioux pony closer until Nathan spun and fired.

Barlow's shot whined past his ear as Holten slipped from the back of his mount. With the distance greatly closed and steady ground under him, Eli fired a single shot that smacked solidly against Barlow's left shoulder.

The outlaw's clavicle shattered into a dozen pieces as the bone absorbed most of the energy of the .44 slug. Bright red blood, from the subclavian artery, gushed out of the wound. The gang leader fell heavily on his buttocks and turned a white-faced, blank expression on the approaching scout.

"Nathan Barlow," Eli began as he dragged the wounded man to his feet. "As a deputy of the town of Eagle Butte, I place you under arrest as an escaped fugitive." The words sounded alien and somewhat fatuous to the scout.

"So," Nathan wheezed, "the righteous man is cast down by Satan's red-hided children and fornicating sinner."

Suddenly the outlaw's pompousness touched Holten's

sense of humor. "We beat you fair and square, Barlow," Eli said laughing. "You shouldn't have killed those Cheyenne boys, or started that fire. You got all the Indians mighty riled. They even forgot they hate whites for a while so they could join us in trackin' you down. Didn't get you this time without firing a shot, but we're gonna give you legal and fair justice, like Marshal Peters would have liked it."

"There is no justice outside of Gawd," Barlow groaned. "I am laid bare and they cast lots for my clothes. They can count all my bones."

The scout stared perplexed at the murderous gang leader for a long time, then hauled back and slugged Nathan Barlow as hard as he could, knocking the bleeding man back to the ground.

"If there's one thing I can't abide," Eli spat, "it's a hypocrite who can't get his Bible quotes right. If you weren't a bunch of filthy, murdering rapists, you wouldn't have fallen into our trap."

"I got a right to a lawyer," Barlow mumbled, a slight note of confused fear in his voice as he tried to stay conscious.

"You'll get what we can supply," Eli responded as he dragged the prison escapee to his feet a second time.

The Reverend Ezekiel Smith brought Circuit Court Judge Louis P. Thornton unerringly to the Sioux camp. The jurist set about preparing his courtroom.

"Who will be the jury, Mister Holten?" Thornton asked as he sat behind a rock that he placed his gavel on.

"The posse took a vote, Your Honor," Eli started. "We

228

feel that since we were all witnesses to one or another of Barlow's crimes, we can't honorably serve as jurors, bein's as we want to testify against them."

"Who, then, shall serve as the jury?" Thornton pressed.

"Big Wolf has graciously made his braves available for this function."

The judge cast a disconcerted look at the grim, stoic warriors, then back at Eli. "They seem of a sound, sober countenance," he managed in a strained voice. Then the jurist cleared his throat and applied his gavel on a small elk hide-covered drum provided for that purpose.

"Good enough, Mister Holten. Have the clerk swear them in and explain their duties. Bring the prisoners."

Tied and shackled, the desperados stumbled across the shallow ford of the Cheyenne River and stood dumbstruck as Eli translated the testimony of the townsfolk to the Sioux and Cheyenne with hand sign and Lakota.

"The case before the court is numerous counts of murder in the first degree, bank robbery, horse stealing, rape, and mayhem," Thornton droned. "How do the defendants plead?"

"Since all of those are capital offenses, Your Honor," Zeke Smith, attorney for the defense answered, "not guilty."

Despite the informality, the trial lasted a good long time, three hours, before the testimony for the prosecution finished. At last, sweating under the broiling fall sun, Opey the bartender mopped at his brow and faced the court.

"The prosecution rests, Your Honor."

Reverend Smith stepped forward for the defense.

"Gentlemen of the jury, fellow townspeople, my distinguished colleague of the prosecution, and Your Honor," Smith began. Several Eagle Butte residents, familiar with the reverend's windy sermons, groaned and prepared themselves for a long and arduous defense. Smith's eyes scanned across the gathered throng of silent men — red and white — as they waited for the minister to present his argument. He smiled, hunched his shoulders in a shrug and raised his hands above his head in submission as he said, "We throw ourselves on the mercy of the court. Defense rests."

"Now wait a minute," Nathan bellowed. He started forward, only to be jerked back by Eli Holten.

The townsfolk clapped wildly while Eli explained the black-robe's statement to the jury.

"Will the jury need time for deliberation?"

Big Wolf listened to the translation, turned to the rest of the jurors and shook his head. He grunted a few more words and Eli turned back to the judge.

"No, Your Honor. After hearing the evidence presented before the court, the jury finds the defendants guilty as charged."

"This ain't fair," Barlow pleaded hysterically to the judge. "We have a right to be judged by our peers, not red savages."

"Be flattered that you have been judged by your betters," Thornton rebuked him. "Besides, the court dismisses all charges brought against Nathan Barlow, Art Hawkins, John Hay, and Harry Lemley."

"What?" Opey blurted.

"Mister Prosecutor, you are out of order," Thornton drawled to Opey. "Those boys are already under sentence of death. I direct acting deputy marshal, Eli Holten, to assist in the execution of the wishes of the court in Kansas. I sentence the rest of the defendants to hang by the neck until they are dead, dead, dead. All motions for retrial are overruled and appeals are denied. Mister Holten, I hope you have plenty of rope."

They had ample rope.

The cottonwoods to the south were sturdy and fairly tall. Six nooses were prepared and swung over stout branches. While the Indians chanted and howled in delight, Bud Greenwood, Leroy McDade, Tim Swanson, their leader, Cooper, and the gunmen as Jace Welles and Jake Day got loaded on bareback horses and tucked under the trees. Rope neckties dangled loosely around their throats with a fair amount of slack, though when separated from their horses, the guests of honor wouldn't quite be able to touch toes to the ground.

"A prayer first, boys," Zeke insisted. All the whitemen present, who didn't have their hands tied, removed their hats and bowed their heads.

"Oh, Lord," Smith prayed fervently. "Make sure the rope don't break."

"Amen," the posse sighed.

A slap to six horse haunches and a blare of rifle fire bolted the mounts out from under the owners, who began a sudden air-borne dance. Six loud snapping sounds filled the late afternoon silence and the executioners cheered as they realized they'd done it right.

"There will be much hardship before you see your enemies dance in the sky," the white bear had told Holten in his dream. There had been great suffering, all right, much loss, and Eli savored helping Nathan Barlow onto the back of a saddleless nag, the murderer's hands tied behind his back.

"You people relish this moment on Satan's earth," Barlow bellowed at the assembled men. "But I go to a better place, in the bosom of Abraham, to my Lord and Gawd, whom I have served throughout my life. I have no shame for my deeds. Gawd has guided me."

"Mister Barlow," Smith called to the doomed man. "It's men like you who give God a bad name."

The townsfolk left the executed men dangle while they draped new ropes between the swaying corpses. Then they brought around the next batch.

The duly appointed deputies of Eagle Butte led the horses carrying Jed and Nathan Barlow, Art Hawkins, John Hay, Harry Lemley, and one of the gunhands to the nooses. The process repeated itself. A prayer, an Amen, and a staccato explosion of gunfire. Horses bolted and the sound of snapping rope and necks brought another round of cheers.

The twelve warriors excitedly danced around, the entertainment of the executions beyond their imaginations.

"Isn't revenge wonderfu?" Amy breathed to the scout as she watched the murderer of her father swing in the breeze, the rope creaking like a squeaky hinge.

Big Wolf led Thunder Woman over to Eli. The two Sioux stood very close and the young maid smiled sweetly. "Tall Bear," the great war chief began, "I have chosen Thunder Woman to be my bride."

Holten smiled and slapped the Oglala leader with an open palm on his shoulder. "You do yourself well," he grunted and gave the healer a wink.

In town once more, the assembled people held another trial for Bart Blackwell. Matt already waited execution. The verdict, equally predictable as that which had come before, came in after only five minutes of deliberation. Judge Thornton rendered the expected sentence.

Behind the marshal's office the town had previously erected a two-holer gallows in anticipation of the Blackwell brothers, so it was with a festive mood that the people of Eagle Butte gathered there late the next day for the hanging of the outlaws.

"Nooooo!" Matthew Blackwell moaned as Eli Holten and three posse men brought him to the small courtyard. "Pleeeease don't ha-ha-ang meee!" Tears streamed down his ashen cheeks and he had gone limp, so that it took the efforts of all three townsmen to drag him up the thirteen steps of the gallows.

"Oh, please, God . . . don't let 'em do it," his brother wailed when his turn came to leave the jail. "We was only havin' a little fun." Snot ran from his nose and the tears gushed hotly. Long before death would have released his sphincters, a large wet stain appeared at Bart's crotch as he voided himself in terror.

More men were summoned from the spectators to hold the boys upright while the properly wrapped nooses were draped over their heads. Spasms of horror set the profligate young men to trembling.

"Bart and Matthew Blackwell, you have been found guilty of murder and sentenced to die. Do you have any last words?" Eli Holten asked, as tradition required.

"Moma . . . Moma," Matthew sobbed.

Eli's hand went to the release lever.

"We're sorry," Bart screamed. "We won't never do it again. We're so sor . . ."

His words got lost in the loud crash of the falling traps.

The round of executions improved the morale of the small Black Hills community. Work began on rebuilding the Thunder Saloon, while the soiled doves worked out of tents on the edge of town. Early evening a few days later, Eli Holten strolled in that direction, humming an idle tune.

He stopped into one tent and Amy Peters greeted him with a warm kiss and groping hands.

"I've decided to answer my life's calling," she explained, undoing Eli's trousers, then sliding to knees to urge the stallion inside to rise and meet her lips. "With Daddy gone, there's no one to be offended."

"The Reverend Smith is going to hold a special service for the Barlow gang," Eli tried to converse between gasps as Amy worked and teased his manhood to its full engorged length. "Bury them proper."

Amy murmured her acknowledgement, tempered somewhat by her muttered words, "They don't deserve it."

"He wants me to introduce him to all the chiefs in the hills," Eli groaned. "Wants to try to convert them."

This time the pretty Amy did not answer but merely began building suction on the scout's life stem. After a long time she extricated herself from his pulsating organ.

"You're going to stay the winter, aren't you, Eli?" Amy asked longingly, looking up with deep blue eyes. "The girls have all agreed. They'd love you to stay. We'll make the winter as toasty as a warm summer day."

The scout smiled nervously, then nodded at the fire that kindled in his log. "I'll stay . . . at least for a while."

But his thoughts turned once again to Texas. Somehow, he thought, winter might prove more exciting there.

THE HOTTEST SERIES IN THE WEST CONTINUES!

BOLT BY CORT MARTIN

#9: BADMAN'S BORDELLO (1127, $2.25)

When the women of Cheyenne cross the local hardcases to exercise their right to vote, Bolt discovers that politics makes for strange bedfellows!

#10: BAWDY HOUSE SHOWDOWN (1176, $2.25)

The best man to run the new brothel in San Francisco is Bolt. But Bolt's intimate interviews lead to a shoot-out that has the city quaking—and the girls shaking!

#11: THE LAST BORDELLO (1224, $2.25)

A working girl in Angel's camp doesn't stand a chance—unless Jared Bolt takes up arms to bring a little peace to the town . . . and discovers that the trouble is caused by a woman who used to do the same!

#12: THE HANGTOWN HARLOTS (1274, $2.25)

When the miners come to town, the local girls are used to having wild parties, but events are turning ugly . . . and murderous. Jared Bolt knows the trade of tricking better than anyone, though, and is always the first to come to a lady in need . . .

Available wherever paperbacks are sold, or order direct from the Publisher. Send cover price plus 50¢ per copy for mailing and handling to Zebra Books, 475 Park Avenue South, New York, N.Y. 10016. DO NOT SEND CASH.